Archibald Geikie

Outlines of Field-Geology

Third Edition

Archibald Geikie

Outlines of Field-Geology
Third Edition

ISBN/EAN: 9783337311469

Printed in Europe, USA, Canada, Australia, Japan

Cover: Foto ©Andreas Hilbeck / pixelio.de

More available books at **www.hansebooks.com**

OUTLINES

OF

FIELD-GEOLOGY.

BY

ARCHIBALD GEIKIE, LL.D., F.R.S.,

Director-General of the Geological Survey of Great Britain and Ireland, lately Murchison Professor of Geology and Mineralogy in the University of Edinburgh, and Director of the Geological Survey of Scotland.

THIRD EDITION:

WITH NUMEROUS ILLUSTRATIONS.

London:

MACMILLAN AND CO.

1882.

RICHARD CLAY & SONS,

BREAD STREET HILL, LONDON, E.C.

And at Bungay, Suffolk.

PREFACE TO THE SECOND EDITION.

At the request of the Lords of the Committee of Privy Council on Education I gave in the month of August, 1876, at South Kensington, two lectures upon geological maps and instruments of surveying. These lectures formed part of a series designed for teachers, and in illustration of the Loan Collection of Scientific Instruments at that time exhibited. Treating the subject allotted to me in what seemed likely to prove the most useful manner, I dwelt more specially upon the methods of observation requisite in ordinary field-geology; and endeavoured to show how by the practice of these methods geological maps and sections, representing in condensed form the facts established by field-work, could be constructed. The lectures were published in pamphlet form later in the autumn of the same year.

A large impression having been sold and the work
having been for some time out of print, the publishers
asked me to allow it to be reprinted in a more perma-
nent shape. I delayed complying with this request until
I could find leisure to revise and extend the lectures. I
have now entirely recast them, and, dropping the original
lecture form, have thrown the matter into chapters, with
distinct headings. So great have been the additions
that the little volume now issued may claim to be a
new and independent work. It retains, however, the un-
pretending elementary character of the original lectures.
My aim has been to write primarily for that large and
increasing body of readers who have made some general
acquaintance with geology, but who, though much interested in the subject, find themselves helpless when
they try to interpret the facts which they meet with in
the field. The practical knowledge of which they feel the
want is not indeed to be gained from books. It must
be sought in quarries and ravines, by hillside and sea-
shore. But hints regarding what should be looked for
and how to set about the search may not be without
some usefulness. And these it is the object of the
following pages to give.

The young geologist into whose hands this little book

may fall will therefore remember that it is not meant as a systematic text-book on geology. It presupposes him to have already read some such text-book, to have acquired a general knowledge of the scope of the science, and to have become in some measure familiar with the facts. Its purpose is to be suggestive to him, rather than didactic; to put him in the way of intelligently observing for himself, rather than to present him with what has already been discovered by others.

COLLEGE, EDINBURGH,

February, 1879.

PREFACE TO THE THIRD EDITION.

A FEW additions and verbal corrections have been made to this edition. The reader will find some portions of the work more fully treated in my *Text-book of Geology*.

28, JERMYN STREET, LONDON,

October, 1882.

CONTENTS.

CONTENTS.

PART II.—IN-DOOR WORK.

LIST OF ILLUSTRATIONS.

OUTLINES OF FIELD-GEOLOGY.

CHAPTER I.

INTRODUCTORY.

To those who are fond of the country and of long rambles there, geology offers many attractions. Few men are so unobservant as not to be struck now and then by at least the more salient features of a landscape. Even in a flat featureless country, the endless and apparently capricious curvings of the sluggish streams may occasionally suggest the question why such serpentine courses should ever have been chosen. But where the ground rises into undulations, and breaks out into hills and crags ; still more, where it towers into rugged mountains, cleft by precipices down which the torrents are ever pouring, and by ravines in the depths of which the hoarse streams ceaselessly murmur, one can hardly escape the natural curiosity to know something about these singular aspects of the landscapes, when and how they arose, and why they should be precisely as they are. For the day is now happily past when the sterner features of the land

B

awakened only a feeling of horror; when they were styled
hideous, and unsightly; when they were never visited
save under the necessities of travel, and were always left
behind with a sense of relief. Relics of these feelings
survive to us in such phrases as wild, savage, uncouth,
with which we still describe that mountain-world, once an
object of awe and fear, now the centre to which a yearly
increasing crowd of visitors repairs for some of the purest
pleasures and most healthful recreation which this world
has to afford. With the growth of an appreciation of
natural scenery in all its forms, rugged as well as gentle,
there has arisen also a desire to know on what causes
these diversities of outline depend. We are not now
content as our fathers were to accept the present aspect
of a country as that which it has worn from the beginning
of time. And even if no intelligible answer can be given
to them, the questions I have referred to will ever and
anon force themselves on our attention.

Nor is it only the larger and more impressive features
of the landscape which suggest such inquiries. A boul-
derstone perched on some slope or on the edge of a
crag, seemingly so perilously poised, that a mere push
with the hand should send it rolling into the plain
below, will raise in our minds the questions why the
block should have stopped where it is, whence did it
come, how was it carried, and what arrested it there? On
either side of a soft, well-cultivated valley we may perhaps
detect, peeping out at intervals from among the wood-
land orchards and cottages, a strong rib of rock, forming everywhere a marked feature, with its grey, lichen-
crusted face, deep fern-hung shadows and tufts of sweet
briar, honeysuckle, or bramble. Its regularity of level

suggests at a distance some artificial land-mark—a road,
or fence, or some ruined rampart. Yet we see on nearer
inspection that it must be a natural feature, and we ask
ourselves why it should have arisen on the face of those
green declivities, and why its course on the one side of
the valley should be so exactly repeated on the other.
Perchance a prominent mound rises from the general
level of a plain, so singularly as to have attracted notice
from the earliest times, and to have become the origin
of a local myth. It seems too large to be due to man's
operations, even if any intelligible reason could be assigned
for his having heaped it together. On the supposition
that it is natural, however, how are we to account for
its existence? What agent could have lifted its
materials and piled them up into that solitary cone?

Again, the merest fragment of stone picked up on any
everyday ramble may furnish questions, for the due answering of which many years of profitable study might be
needed. A piece of limestone, for example, may show us
on its fractured surface abundant fragments of corals and
shells. With a little inquiry it may not be difficult to
ascertain the source of the stone, and to visit the rock
in place. We may there find a thick bed of limestone,
crowded throughout with similar organisms, and extending
for miles across the country. It would need but a slender
acquaintance with modern science to make us feel assured
that this limestone must represent an old sea-bottom once
thickly covered with living things. We might muse on
the strange vicissitudes of nature, wherein the busy floor
of a former ocean should have been changed into a land
" made blithe with plough and harrow," and might ask
ourselves how and when these revolutions were effected.

In the course of another walk we might stumble upon a bit of stone made up of rounded pebbles cemented together, as if a handful of gravel from some river-side had been hardened into stone. Could we trace this fragment also to its original locality, we should find it to have formed part of a larger bed or mass of what is called conglo-merate or puddingstone, and we should recognize still more the exact resemblance of the constituent stones of this rock to the shingle of a sea-shore, or the gravel of a river-bed. We could not for a moment doubt that the rock must be merely so much compacted water-worn gravel. But where lay the water by which these stones were rounded and polished? Was it the sea, or a lake, or a river? What was the aspect of the country then, and through what cycle of change has it past to reach its present condition?

Thus even to one who knows no geology, the problems of the science are presented at every turn and in every country ramble. When, however, some acquaintance with this science has been gained, the number of questions which arise for solution rapidly increases, and with their growth there augments also the power of answering them, or at least the pleasure of seeking for their solution. The observer, as he finds his knowledge and consequently his confidence enlarged, discovers on the one hand that facts which he took for granted, and which never raised in his mind any question or difficulty, now demand some ex-planation, and, on the other, that he has to disabuse him-self of many prejudices or notions which grew up in his mind, he cannot tell when or how. For example, it never used to occur to him that there was anything especially deserving of notice in the fact, that the stones of an old

building almost invariably have lost their sharp edge, and
in many cases are crumbling and honey-combed.   But he
now observes these aspects, and derives from their study
another pleasure to be added to the many which an interesting ruin yields to every one.   He notes what kinds
of stones decay most, on which aspect of the building
the weathering is most advanced, and endeavours to
ascertain on what circumstances the disintegration seems
to have depended.   For he recognizes that the walls of
a building may be likened to the sides of a crag or
precipice, and that in contemplating the progress of decay
in a human edifice, he can learn not a little respecting
the laws which govern the disintegration of the mountains.   Again, he no doubt began with the common
popular belief that the striking features of a landscape,
notably its crags and ravines, are to be referred directly
to the operation of earthquakes and former convulsions
of nature.   Slowly and perhaps with some difficulty he
rids himself of the incubus of this prejudice.   He re-
fuses any longer to be bound by preconceived theory
or explanation, but insists on being allowed to judge of
each instance on its own merits and to reason upon it
with reference to all its surroundings.

   If after having familiarized his eyes with the outward
aspect and inner geological relations of his own district,
the observer extends his journeys into other regions, he
carries with him an added power of enjoyment in every
country through which he may wander.   He finds that
an acquaintance with geology, far from blinding him to the
softer beauties or wilder grandeur of a landscape, really
quickens his perception of these charms.   Practice enables
him to take in at a glance the dominant features, and to

range the others in their orderly subordinate places, so that the harmony of the whole is seized, and the impression which it makes is fixed upon the mind. If I may be allowed to make the comparison, it is with the appreciation of scenery as with the cultivation of music. Most listeners of average education and intelligence thoroughly enjoy a sonata of Beethoven ; they listen to a harmonious variety of sound, and perhaps at the close awake almost out of dreamland. And yet, high as is their enjoyment, it can hardly equal that of the musician who recognizes, as movement succeeds movement, the skill and genius of the composer who could so vary and amplify some simple theme, and while seeming to abandon himself to a tumultuous torrent of sound could keep every portion of the work under the strictest rules of art, and with a breadth and harmony that bind the composition into one magnificent whole.

Should the traveller find himself with leisure sufficient not merely to look at the scenery but to examine the rocks which form its groundwork, he will again find his experience at home stand him in good stead and give fresh interest to his journey. He will encounter other and often better illustrations of phenomenon with which he has already become practically familiar. He will perhaps meet with facts which throw a bright light on questions which had long puzzled him in his own country. Or he may see for the first time, and with a joy which he alone can experience, an example of some piece of geological structure which he has known only from books, but which he now and for ever vividly realizes.

In all this it is not needful that he should claim to be a geologist. He may not consider his observations

worthy of attention from professed geologists, or he
may have neither time nor inclination to publish them.
But none the less does he enjoy the refreshment, alike
bodily and mental, which geological work in the field
brings with it. Should he, however, deem it proper to
give the world the benefit of his labours, he may have
the satisfaction of adding to the sum of knowledge, and
of eliciting the thanks of geologists who will gladly
admit him of their number. More especially should he
be encouraged to publish his observations when they
relate to unvisited or little known regions, or to tracts
where he has enjoyed exceptional advantages for studying
geological phenomena.

But how is this geological experience to be acquired?
How often do we meet with men who have read extensively in geology, yet if they are set down among the
rocks find themselves hopelessly adrift, and after some
despairing efforts to recognize in nature what seems so
clear in the diagrams of a text-book, give up the pursuit
in disgust. On the other hand, how constantly are men
to be encountered who labour under the delusion that
nature is as easily read as the manual whose pages they
have so often skimmed over, and who proceed at once
to quarry, hillside, or mountain, and explain its geological
features with much more confidence than those would
pretend to do who have made the subject their prolonged
study. It is not from books alone that a man can
acquire that practical acquaintance with geology which
will minister so much to his elevation and enjoyment.
He must betake himself to nature from the first. His
lessons in the field should accompany his lessons from
the text-book or lecture-room. In many cases he must

grope his way without guide or assistance. His progress
will be slow, but in the end he may find that it has been
none the less sure and pleasant, and that, through this
very tardiness of his advance, he has been compelled to
master thoroughly every foothold of the way. The
following chapters are offered for his help. They are
not to stand in .the place of a systematic text-book, of
which he will find still constant need. But still less are
they to be looked at as in any way a substitute for practical observation in the field. Their aim is to point out
how observations may be made, what kinds of data
should be looked for, what sort of evidence should be
sought to establish a conclusion, and what deductions
may be drawn from particular facts. In short, they are
to be regarded as sign-posts pointing out some of the
high-ways and bye-ways of geological inquiry, but
leaving the reader to perform the journey in his own
fashion. Their object will be fully realized if they induce
him to find so much interest in the pursuit as to adopt
it as a frequent solace for his leisure hours. But they
are so arranged that it is hoped they may not be found
without service to young geologists, who, whether at
home or abroad, would fain devote themselves with
energy to the task of geological investigation.

The term Field-Geology, which I have selected as
expressive of my subject, points then, to practical work
in the open field, as distinguished from the researches
which may be carried on in the library or laboratory. I
wish to describe some of the methods by which a
geologist obtains his information regarding the nature,
position, arrangement, and history of the rocks of a
country. Such practical observation evidently underlies

all solid research in geology. He who would pursue the
theoretical parts of the science must either himself lay
a foundation in good thorough field-work, or take advantage of the foundation which has, in this respect, been
laid for him by others.

Field-geology may be pursued with various aims and
in various ways. To some men it is little more than
another name for holiday-making in the country—fresh
air, healthy exercise, new or old charms of scenery, and
a bag full of "specimens" to attest the scientific nature
of the work. To others it is the solace and delight of
busy lives, furnishing them not only with bright intervals
of escape to the country, but with materials for much
profitable thought and study when the ordinary duties
and cares of life confine them to their work in town. To
other men, again, it is itself the main occupation of life,
whether they cultivate it for its own sake, or with a
view to the economic applications of which it is
susceptible.

There are few countries or districts where field-geology
may not be cultivated, and where its healthful influence
as an educational instrument may not be tested. A few
days of intelligently guided observation in the field are
worth far more to a pupil than many weeks of lectures
and reading. But we seldom hear of such practical
instruction, mainly because the teachers never received
it, and have not had time, inclination, or opportunity to
develop it for themselves.

PART I.

OUT-OF-DOOR WORK.

CHAPTER II.

FIRST ESSAYS IN FIELD-WORK.

THE direction in which the first essays of the observer in the field should be made, must depend mainly upon the nature of the district in which he finds himself situated. Under the most unfavourable circumstances, as for instance in a wide cultivated plain, with not a single quarry or natural opening to show even the nature of the formations underneath, he may nevertheless discover something to engage his attention. Thus, he may find useful employment in watching the operations of the streams which flow sluggishly through his neighbourhood, their meanderings and the efforts they make to straighten their courses, their varying quantity of mud, the effects of floods, the evidence of successive deposits, and heightening of the flood-plain. But it will seldom happen that he cannot in some way gain access to the geological formations below the surface, and even in a flat and featureless region obtain a series of facts which will enable him to reason as to the history of the region, and to decide whether the plain has been formed by the stream, or on the floor of some ancient lake, or perchance on the bed of the sea.

Where, however, numerous openings, either natural or artificial, expose the strata underneath, the observer need be at no loss for abundant material for profitable field work. Should some of these strata be eminently fossiliferous, that is, crowded with the remains of once living plants or animals, they will almost certainly attract his earliest attention. Probably in the majority of cases men have been led to the study of geology by first becoming interested in the organic remains which they could collect for themselves, carry home as "specimens," and afterwards thoughtfully question as to their structure and history. No doubt the mere gathering of the fossils is the first and final achievement of a very large proportion of enthusiastic beginners. Even, however, if the pursuit has had no other advantage than that of affording ample exercise in the open air, it is perhaps not less beneficial than many of the time honoured forms of out-of-door recreation.

But a man may gain much more than healthful amusement from fossil-hunting. He begins, let us suppose, by trying to get hold of as many varieties, and as perfect specimens as he can find by the most patient search. But the mere pleasure of the pursuit soon begets a desire to know more about the fossils. If they are plants, the collector strives to ascertain their names, and may be content perhaps if he can write upon them their proper Latin or Greek appellations. Possessed, however, of a real desire for knowledge, he seeks to ascertain what are their affinities with the living vegetation of to-day. By reading, by visiting museums, and by careful observation along the hedgerows or in botanic gardens, he endeavours to realize what the leaves and stems, which he finds in the solid stone, really were when they waved bright and green in the air long ages ago. The information he can glean as to their probable botanical grade and habit, leads him to re-examine, with greater care, the circumstances under which they lie in the rock. He finds, perhaps, that they occur more particularly in one stratum, which we shall suppose consists of thin leaves or laminæ of a kind of hardened clay. It is on splitting up these laminæ that he unfolds the fossil plants. Each layer seems entirely covered with impressions of leaves, stems, fruits, or other parts of the ancient vegetation; but the fossils are all fragmentary, though well preserved. They remind him of the sheddings of trees after some early autumnal frost; the fine layers of hardened silt, on which they lie, recall the laminæ of mud which he has observed in the bottom of a pond or dried-up pool; and in the end, he concludes with some confidence that his fossil-bearing stratum was once the floor of some inland sheet of water, into which the leaves of the neighbouring woodlands were periodically shed. If he has ascertained that the plants are more nearly allied to those of a warmer region than the vegetation now flourishing in the locality, he allows himself to speculate on the probability that a warmer climate once prevailed in his own country.

The remains of animals, however, are immensely more abundant among the rocks than those of plants. The observer is much more likely, therefore, to begin by lighting upon some stratum full of shells, crinoids, corals, or even with bones of fishes, and perhaps of reptiles. If he is not satisfied merely with forming a collection of these remains and having them rightly named, but wishes to learn what they have to tell him about ancient types of life and old conditions of physical geography, he addresses himself to the task by endeavouring to find the nearest analogies in the living world to the fossil forms which he has disinterred from the rocks. Patiently he tries to reconstruct the skeleton of which he has found the scattered bones. He learns to recognize the fragment of a shell or other fossil, and can assign it to its place in the complete organism. While the structure and zoological relations of the fossils afford him inexhaustible stores of employment, he cannot shut his eyes to the circumstances in which these fossils occur, and to the light which they cast on the history of the rocks. Corals, crinoids, and marine types of molluscan life bring before him an old sea-floor, and though the locality where his leisure hours are thus sedulously spent may now lie far in the heart of a country, with venerable trees and hedgerows, old farmsteads and roads, all bearing witness to the peaceful cultivation of centuries, the sight of that rock with its crowded fossils is as sure evidence of the former presence of the sea over the whole landscape, as if he heard there even now the murmur of the waves.

But the observer's lot may be cast in a district where no fossils are to be found. There may be nothing in the rocks themselves to attract notice, nothing likely to inspire a taste for geology or to furnish nutriment for a taste already existent. It is remarkable, however, in what apparently unfavourable circumstances an appetite for

scientific pursuits can not only exist but flourish. Let
us suppose that the district in question consists of stratified rocks, like sandstones and shales, and that these
strata are exposed to view in numerous quarries and
natural sections. The varying composition of the beds,
their order of succession, their changes in character as
they are traced over the country, their influence upon
the contour of the ground, the glimpses they afford of
an ancient geography very different from that of the
district to-day, and the manner in which they have been
tilted up, curved, and broken since the time of their
original formation—these, and a thousand other particulars, will eventually give even barren and seemingly
repulsive rocks a charm which the richly fossiliferous
deposits of the observer's later experience may never
possess. If, on the other hand, the rocks are crystalline
—granites, schists, and other similar masses, or basalts,
tuffs, and other volcanic accumulations, the geologist,
who begins work among them will almost of necessity
devote himself to the mineralogical and structural side of
the science. He may be first attracted by pretty minerals,
—sparkling felspars, well crystallized and variously
coloured quartzes, glittering micas, and many more. And
doubtless the temptation to collect them, if it once arises
within him, will not be likely to diminish, so long as his
taste for geological pursuits lasts, and as he finds himself
face to face with the minerals in the field. Pursued not
as the hobby of a collector, but as an important branch
of the sciences which deal with the architecture of the
globe, mineralogy becomes a singularly fascinating study.
I shall have occasion in later chapters to allude to some
of its attractions. Should the observer be led from the

minerals to the investigation of the rocks among which
they lie, he will find himself in presence of some of the
most interesting problems in geology.   Some of these
crystalline rocks are amongst the oldest of the globe;
their origin is linked with the earth's early history, they
are the witnesses of the power of that internal heat which
has played so notable a part in the growth of the solid
land.   As a rule, too, the districts where they occur are
more rugged than those which the fossiliferous formations
overspread : hence they present everywhere crags, knobs
and bosses of rock, as well as the more continuous sections of water-courses.   By these frequent exposures the
successive bands of rock can be traced across the district; their variations in breadth, in composition and in
mineral contents can be followed ; and their intercalations,
curvatures, fractures, and veins, can be unravelled, so as
to reveal, more or less clearly, the structural plan of the
whole region.

In most places, save on the face of precipices and
steep declivities, the rocks which form the framework of
a country are more or less concealed by various superficial accumulations.   Even should he never set himself
to the study of the underlying formations, the observer
may find ample scope for inquiry in these upper deposits.
In one region he will encounter thick masses of earth or
loam, containing here and there the bones of long extinct
mammals.   In another quarter he may meet with sheets
of gravel, perched on the sides of valleys high above the
present streams, yet evidently themselves of fluviatile
origin, and containing scattered rude implements of
human workmanship.   In yet a third locality he will
find a mass of clay, stuck full of stones with their surfaces

polished and scratched like the rocks below a Swiss glacier, and he will learn that these striated stones and the clay containing them have once likewise been under a sheet of ice. In short he will soon perceive that in every one of the many varieties of superficial deposits there is a story to be made out, and that it is worth his while to decipher it.

Lastly, it may chance that the beginner is so situated as to be able to watch the actual visible progress of geological changes. His home may be by the margin of a river liable to occasional floods, and always bearing onward past him its burden of mud from the distant hills. No better training in geological observation could he desire than that which is supplied by a careful and methodical study of the operations of a river. Its times of flood and of low water, the proportion of mineral substances in its water from month to month, the way in which the sediment is disposed of, the action of the river on its banks, here cutting down and there heaping up, the relation of the form of the channel to the rocks through which it has been cut, now a ravine, now a waterfall, here a rapid, there a lake-like reach—these and many other points in the physics of a river furnish endless material of ever fresh interest. The stream has its moods like a living thing; no two years of its operations are exactly alike, and it seems always to have surprises in store for us, though we have watched it for years and are familiar with it under every aspect.

Even more fortunate is the observer whose dwelling lies not only near a river but within reach of the sea. Even if the shore be low and sandy, he can watch the breakers as they come tumbling in upon the beach, and mark how the colour of the water changes as it drags back the sand in its recoil. The sight of this ceaseless grinding impresses him, as hardly any other can do so well, with the way in which the boulders and gravel are reduced to the state of sand and spread over the sea-floor, there to lay the foundations of the land of future ages. But should the coast be rocky, he may congratulate himself on having been placed in a kind of geological paradise. Hardly anywhere else will he meet with the same facilities for observation. The beach serves as a platform on which the rocks are exposed for his study, and which is swept clean for him twice every day by the tides. He may devote himself to the investigation of the rocks themselves, their contents and history, or he may observe the way in which they yield to the attacks made upon them by the sea on one side and by the air, rain, frost, and springs on the other.

We may conclude, therefore, that there must be very few parts of the world where some kind of field-geology cannot be pursued. If the beginner who has read enough in the science to make him desirous of becoming himself an observer, finds it hopelessly impossible to extract any information or interest from his surroundings, he will probably be right in suspecting that the fault lies in himself, and not in them. Perhaps the chapters which follow may suggest some method of overcoming his difficulty.

C

CHAPTER III.

THE nature and extent of a geologist's accoutrements will, of course, be regulated by the kind of work he proposes to undertake, and the character of the rocks among which he is to be engaged. If his object be the collection of specimens of minerals, rocks or fossils, he will require one sort of apparatus : if it be the study of the geological structure of the region, he will provide himself with another sort. It must be distinctly understood at the outset, that the popular idea that a geologist must necessarily be one who amasses stones and comes home with a fresh burden from every excursion, is a popular but rather mischievous delusion.

Field-geology does not mean and need not include the collecting of specimens. Consequently a formidable series of hammers and chisels, a capacious wallet with stores of wrapping paper and pill-boxes, are not absolutely and always required. Rock-specimens and fossils are best collected after the field-geologist has made some progress with his examination of a district. He can then begin to see what rocks really deserve to be illustrated by specimens, and in what strata the search for fossils may be most advantageously conducted. He may have to undertake the collecting himself, or he may be able to employ a trained assistant, and direct him to the localities whence specimens are to be taken. But in the first instance, his own efforts must be directed to the investigation of the geological structure of the region. The specimens required for his purpose in the early stages of his work do not involve much trouble. He can detach them and carry them off as he goes, while he leaves the full collection to be made afterwards.

It is of paramount importance that the field-geologist should go to his work as lightly equipped as possible. His accoutrements should be sufficient for their purpose, and eminently portable. The reader may judge of the portability which may be secured, when he learns that he may carry on his person, at the same moment, all the instruments necessary for a geological investigation, even in the detailed manner adopted in the Geological Survey of this country, and that yet, although a fully-equipped field-geologist, he need not betray his occupation by any visible implement. The want of such tokens of his craft often greatly perplexes rustic observers to whom his movements are a fruitful source of speculation. He may find himself, for instance, taken at different times and places for postman, doctor, farmer, cattle-dealer, travelling-showman, country-gentleman, gamekeeper, poacher, temperance-lecturer, gauger, clergyman, play-actor, and a generally suspicious character. One of my colleagues in the Geological Survey, who had just taken quarters in a village, was watched for some time by the police, under the belief that he had been concerned in a recent burglary.[1]

---

[1] On one occasion, in company with a Survey colleague, I reached a straggling village in the East of Fife, just after a travelling show

1. *The Map.*—Unless the geological work to be done merely consists in visiting already known ground and making detailed notes, or collecting specimens there, it is of the utmost consequence to obtain as good a map of the region as can be had. Not merely does the observer find the advantage of the topographical guide over the ground, but, as I shall point out in a succeeding chapter, he cannot, in many cases, satisfactorily work out the geological relations of the rocks unless he possesses a map on which to place, in their proper geographical position, the notes he makes at each locality. Hence if he cannot procure a map, or if he is at work in a country which has not yet been topographically surveyed, he may find himself compelled to make a map for himself with as near an approach to accuracy as the means at his command will admit.

2. *The Hammer.*—This is the chief instrument of the field-geologist. He ought at first to use it constantly, and seldom trust himself to name a rock until he has broken a fragment from it, and compared the fresh with the weathered surface. Most rocks yield so much to the action of the weather as to acquire a decomposed, crumbling crust, by which the true colour, texture, and composition of the rock itself may be entirely concealed. Two rocks, of which the outer crusts are similar, may

had entered it. The villagers were still standing at their doors, discussing the character of the new arrival, when we passed them. Of course we were naturally supposed to form a kind of rear-guard of the cavalcade ; but we had the satisfaction of hearing one old woman remark to her neighbour, as we brushed past them, " Na, noo, arena' thae twa decent-looking chields to be play-acting blackguards ?"

differ greatly from each other in essential characters. Again, two rocks may assume a very different aspect externally, and yet may show an identity of composition on a freshly-fractured internal surface. The hammer, therefore, is required to detach this outer deceptive crust. If heavy enough to do this, it is sufficient for the purpose; any additional weight is unnecessary and burdensome. A hammer, of which the head weighs one pound or a few ounces more is quite massive enough for all the ordinary requirements of the field-geologist. When he proceeds to collect specimens he needs a hammer of two or three pounds, or even more, in weight, and a small, light chipping hammer, to trim the specimens and reduce them in bulk, without running a too frequent risk of shattering them to pieces.

  . Hardly any two geologists agree as to the best shape of hammer; much evidently depending upon the individual style in which each observer wields his tool. This (Fig. 1) is the form which, after long experience we have found in the Geological Survey to be on the whole the best. A hammer formed after this pattern combines, as may be observed, the uses both of a hammer and a chisel. With the broad, heavy, or square end, we can break off a fragment large enough to show the internal grain of a rock. With the thin, wedge-shaped, or chisel-like end, we can split open shales, sandstones, schists, and other fissile rocks. This cutting or splitting edge should be at a right angle to the axis of the shaft. If placed upright or in the same line with the shaft, much of its efficiency is lost, especially in wedging off plates of shale or other rocks.

A hammer shaped as I recommend serves at times for

other than purely geological purposes. On steep grassy slopes, where the footing is precarious, and where there is no available hold for the hand, the wedge-like end of the hammer may be driven firmly into the turf, and the geologist may thereby let himself securely down or pull himself up.

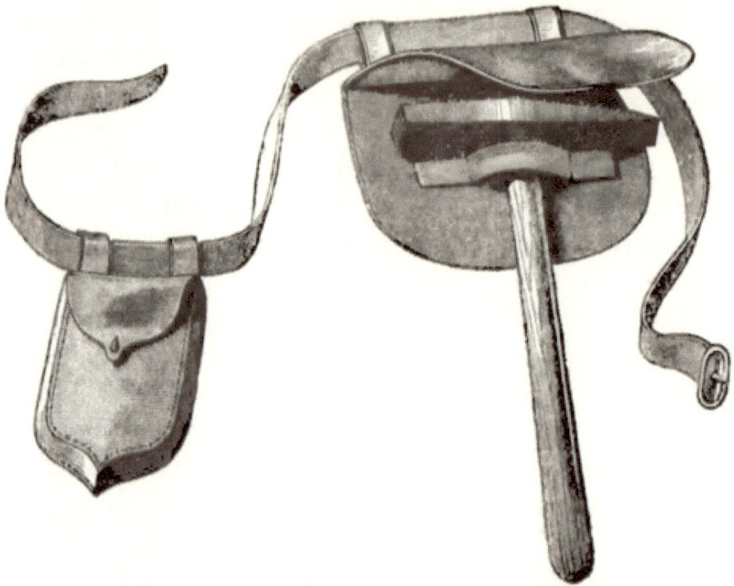

FIG. 1.—Geological hammer, compass-case, and belt.

The most generally convenient way of carrying the hammer is to have it in a leather sheath suspended from the waist-belt. The hammer hangs at the left side under the coat, the inside of which is kept from being cut or soiled by the protecting outer flap of the sheath. Some geologists prefer to carry the belt across the shoulders outside, and the hammer suspended at the back. Others provide themselves with strong canvas coat-pockets and carry the hammer there.

3. *The Lens.*—Even the most sharp-sighted observer is the better of the aid supplied to him by a good magnifying-glass. For field-work a pocket lens with two powers is usually sufficient. One glass should have a large field for showing the general texture of a rock, its component grains or crystals, and the manner of their arrangements; the other glass should be capable of making visible the fine striæ on a crystal, and the minuter ornament on the surface of a fish-scale or other fossil organism. Applied to the weathered crust of a rock, the lens often enables the observer to detect indications of composition and texture, which the fresh fracture of the rock does not reveal. It sometimes suffices to decide whether a puzzling fine-grained rock should be referred to the igneous or the aqueous series, and consequently how that rock is to be coloured on the map.

4. *The Compass.*—Any ordinary pocket compass will suffice for most of the requirements of the field-geologist. Should he need to take accurate bearings, however, a small portable azimuth compass will be found useful. This is the instrument employed in the Geological Survey. It is carried in a leather case or pocket hung from the waist-belt, on the side of the body opposite to the hammer. (Fig. 1.) The directions of the dip and strike of rocks, the trend of dislocations and dykes, the line of boundaries, escarpments, and other geological features are observed accurately, and noted on the spot at the time of observation, either on the map or in the note-book. A convenient instrument for light and rapid surveys, or reconnaissances, combines the compass and the

next instrument I have to describe—the clinometer. I shall refer to it again.

5. *The Clinometer*, or dip-measurer, is employed to find the angle at which strata are placed to the horizon—an important observation in the investigation of the geological structure of a country, and one having frequently a special economic value, as, for instance, when it points out the depth to which a well or mine must be sunk. Various patterns have been proposed and used for this instrument. Formerly a spirit-level was commonly employed. But apart from the difficulty of rapid adjustment for the

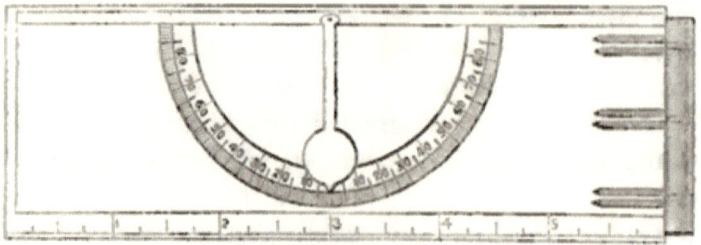

FIG. 2.—Clinometer.

requirements of the field, the spirit levels in the clinometers were apt to get broken. A much more portable and serviceable form of clinometer may be made by the geologist himself. It consists of two thin leaves of wood, each two inches broad and six inches long, neatly hinged together, so as to open out and form a foot rule when required. On the inside of one of these leaves a small brass pendulum is so fixed that when it swings freely and hangs vertically, it forms an angle of 90°, with the upper edge of the leaf to which it is attached. An arc, graduated to 90° on each side of the vertical, is drawn on the wood, or on paper or brass fastened to the wood, so that when the leaf is moved on either side, the exact number of degrees of inclination is shown by the pendulum on the graduated arc. The corresponding face of the opposite leaf is hollowed out just enough to let the two leaves fit closely, and keep the pendulum in its place when the instrument is not in use. This form of clinometer, made of boxwood and bound with brass, may be obtained of instrument makers.[1] It is light and strong, and its durability may be understood from the fact that the instrument which I carry in the field, though it has been in constant use for more than twenty years, is as true and serviceable as ever.

If at any time the geologist has occasion to lighten his equipment for some long mountain expedition, where every additional ounce of weight begins to tell by the end of the day, and where, therefore, for the sake of doing as much and holding out as long as possible, he should carry nothing that is not absolutely needful for his purpose, he may advantageously combine the pocket-compass and clinometer, in the one instrument to which I have already alluded. This convenient instrument is about the size of an ordinary gold watch. It consists of a thin, round, flat metal case, shaped like that of a watch, and covered either with a common watch-glass, or still better, with a flat disc of strong glass. Instead of figures for the hours and minutes, the white enamelled face of this geological watch is that of a common pocket-

---

[1] Messrs. Troughton and Simms, London, Mr. J. Bryson, Edinburgh, and Messrs. Spencer and Son, Dublin, supply this and the other instruments referred to in the text.

compass. But the interval between each of the four
cardinal points is divided into 90°. On the central
pivot, just underneath the needle, a small brass pendulum
is placed, and a straight-edge of metal is soldered on one
side of the outer rim of the watch-case in such a position
that the instrument will stand on it if need be, and the
pendulum will then point to zero. A simple piece of
mechanism passing through the handle enables the
observer to throw the needle off the pivot, or let it
down, as he may require.

6. *The Note-Book and Pencils.*—As it is impossible for
a field-geologist to remember the details of all the observations he makes on the ground, or to insert them on a
map, he regards a good note-book as an essential part of
his apparatus. From the nature of his work he has
frequently occasion to make rough sections, or diagrams,
and if possessed of the power of sketching, he has
abundant opportunity of aiding the progress of his
researches by jotting down the outlines of some cliff,
mountain, or landscape. Hence his note-book should
not be a mere pocket memorandum-book. A convenient
size, uniting the uses of a common note-book and a
sketch-book, is seven inches long by four-and-a-quarter
inches broad. Let me remark in passing that perhaps
no accomplishment will be found so useful by the field-
geologist as a power of rapid and effective sketching from
nature. If he has this power in any degree, he ought
sedulously to cultivate it. Even though he may never
produce a picture, he can catch and store up in his note-
book impressions and outlines which no mere descriptions could recall, and which may be of the highest value
in his subsequent field-work. This is true of ordinary

detailed surveys, and still more of rapid reconnaissances which may have their ultimate usefulness enormously increased if the observer can seize with his pencil and carry away, the forms of surface as well as the geological relations of the region through which his traverse lies.

As every device which saves labour and time in the field, or which adds to the clearness of the work, is deserving of attention, I would refer here to the use of variously-coloured pencils for expressing at once, upon map or note-book, the different rock-masses which may occur in a district. Water-colours are of course ulti- mately employed for representing the geological .forma- tions on the finished map. But a few bits of coloured pencils carried in his pocket save the geologist much needless writing in the field. To a red dot or line he attaches a particular meaning, and he places it on his map without further explanation than the local pecu- liarities of the place may require.

Such are the few prime instruments required in field- geology. We may add others from time to time, ac- cording to the nature of the work, which in each region will naturally suggest the changes that may be most advantageously made. A small bottle of weak hydro- chloric acid, carried in a protecting wooden box, or case, is sometimes of use in testing for carbonates, particularly in regions where rocks of different characters come to resemble each other on their weathered surfaces. When Sir William Logan was carrying on the survey of the Laurentian limestones of Canada, he received much help from what he called his " limestone spear." This was a sharp-pointed bit of iron fixed to the end of a pole or a walking-stick. He enlisted farmers and others

in his operations, instructed them in the use of the
spear, and obtained information which gave him a good
general notion of the distribution of the limestone. The
spear was thrust down through the soil until it struck the
rock below. It was then pulled up, and the powder of
stone adhering to the iron point was tested with acid.
If, after trying a number of places all round, the observer
uniformly obtained a brisk effervescence when the acid
drop fell on the point of his spear, he inferred that the
solid limestone existed below, and noted the fact on his
map accordingly.

When the Geological Survey was busy with the great
Wealden area of the south-east of England, my colleagues used what they nicknamed a " geological cheese-
taster." It was indeed a kind of large cheese-taster,
fixed to the end of a long stick. This implement was
thrust down, and portions of the subsoil and of the clays
or sands beneath were pulled up and examined. Similar
devices must obviously suggest themselves according
to the nature of the work in different districts and
countries.

In the course of his observations in the field the
geologist will meet with rocks, as to the true nature of
which he may not be able to satisfy himself at the time.
He should in such cases detach a fresh chip from some
less weathered part of the mass and examine it further at
home. Detailed methods of investigation, which may
be pursued with all the conveniences of a laboratory in
town, are not possible to him in the country. But he
may subject his specimens to analysis in two ways, and
obtain valuable, and perhaps sufficient, information as to
their characters. He can easily fit up for himself a

small and portable blowpipe box, apparatus for preparing
rocks, minerals, and fossils for examination, and a microscope with which to examine them.   In Part II. of this
little volume I shall enter into some details regarding
these indoor employments of the field-geologist, and
show how the apparatus may be put to practical use.

7. *The Blowpipe Box* should contain as much of the
most useful apparatus as the space will admit, consistently
with the whole box being easily packed into a portmanteau. The reader will find a list of the more essential
articles in Chapter XVI. By means of the blowpipe
it is often possible to determine the nature of a doubtful
mineral or rock, and to ascertain the proportion of metal
in an ore. A young geologist should take with him to
the field only the most essential apparatus and re-agents ;
he will gradually come to see by practice what additions
he may best make to his equipment. Details on this
subject will be found in Chapter XVI.

8. *Rock-slicing Apparatus.*—Portable forms of slicing
and polishing machines are now to be procured, though
even the lightest of them add considerably to the
traveller's baggage. The field-geologist may succeed,
however, in preparing his slices by chipping thin splinters
from the rock and reducing them in the manner described
in Chapter XVII., where instructions are given which it
is hoped will enable him to supply himself with a microscopic slice of any rock he may encounter in the field.
The labour involved in this process is well bestowed,
for by means of the microscope, more than by any
other method, he obtains an insight into the internal
texture and arrangement of the rocks with which he
is dealing. He sees what are the component minerals

of a rock, and how they are built up to form the mass in which they occur.   He likewise can detect many of the changes which these minerals have undergone, and he thus obtains a clue into some of the metamorphic pro-cesses by which the rocks of the earth's crust have been altered.

9. *Microscope.*—This instrument should be, like the rest, as portable as possible.   For most geological pur-poses high powers are not required, consequently a small microscope is sufficient.   Two powers $1\frac{1}{2}$ and $\frac{1}{2}$ inch focal length are extemely useful, and for the requirements of work in the field are quite adequate.   An instrument with fairly good glasses of these powers, magnifying from 30 to about 300 diameters, according to the arrangement of object-glasses and eye-pieces, may be had of some London makers for £5.

It is sometimes of service, when working in a district where microscopic rock-sections are required, to carry a small collection of microscopic slices of selected or typical rocks or minerals, for purposes of comparison.   A series of fifty or one hundred slices can be packed in a box a few inches square.[1]

---

[1] Typical series of this kind may be had from Fuess, of Berlin, or from Tennant or Gregory, London ; or Bryson, Edinburgh.

CHAPTER IV.

IN the foregoing list of a field-geologist's accoutrements, the map was put first. The propriety of assigning it this place of honour will be admitted when the real meaning and importance of a geological map are recognized, and when the observer can carry with him the map on which he himself has traced the geological boundary-lines. A published geological map is a valuable guide when it can be had, but in the field-geologist's eyes its importance is but secondary compared with the map which contains perhaps the substance of his work for weeks or months together.

The results obtained by the geologist in the field, from his investigation of the rocks, may be set down either in writing, or in maps and sections. No one can follow the practical pursuit of the science without being conscious how much his work gains in precision when he is compelled to put it down upon a map. Not only is his information made more accurate, when he requires to trace the exact lines of geological boundary, but he is led to search in nooks and corners, of which he would not otherwise have suspected the existence, and thus he acquires a thoroughness of grasp attainable in no other

way. The best field-geology is of that kind which careful
and minute map-making requires. It is not, of course,
imperative that an actual survey should be made by the
geologist; but he must proceed in such a way that his
observations, if tabulated and placed upon a map, would
make that map a good geological one.

Since, then, the kind of work required in the preparation of geological maps illustrates most completely the
nature and methods of field-geology, I shall describe the
construction of these maps as practised in this country.
The reader will bear in mind that, though he may never
draw a geological boundary line, nor take any part in a
geological survey, he cannot attain excellence in the
practical pursuit of geology in the field, without going
through the training which, if need be, would qualify him
for becoming a professional geologist. How this should
be the case will, I hope, become clear in the sequel.

Let us first consider what a "geological map" is. The
meaning now attached to this term differs very much from
that with which it was associated not very many years ago.
In the early days of geology, those who devoted themselves
to this branch of science were mineralogists, rather than
what we should now call geologists. They termed their
subject "geognosy," meaning thereby to indicate their
object to be the increase of their knowledge of the
minerals and rocks of the earth. They constructed what
they called "geognostical maps," on which the positions
of marked varieties of minerals and rocks were shown,
but without any attempt at accurate, or even sometimes
approximate, boundary lines, and with no hint whatever
of geological structure, which we now regard as one of
the chief objects of geological maps.

A perfect geological map should represent—1st. A full and accurate topography, with the form of the surface and heights in contour-lines, shading, or otherwise. The Ordnance Survey maps of Britain on the scale of six inches to a mile may be taken as an admirable example. 2nd. All geological deposits, from the most recent to the most ancient, which may occur in the district embraced by the map, with their boundary lines accurately traced, and the relation of their distribution to the external form of the ground clearly depicted. 3rd. The geological structure of the region, that is, the relation of the rocks to each other, their inclination downwards from the surface, their curvatures and dislocations; in short, all particulars necessary to enable a geologist to apprehend the manner in which the rocks of the crust of the earth beneath the region in question have been built up. 4th. Information which may have special economic value, such as the nature and distribution of the soils, the position of available building materials, the direction, thickness, and extent of ores, coal-seams, or other useful minerals, the best sources of water supply, &c.

To fulfil these various requirements the map must evidently be on not too small a scale. If the scale is small, the attempt to crowd a great deal of information into the map may result in confusion of detail, and most of the beauty and usefulness of the work may be lost. In such cases it is better, where practicable, to subdivide the labour, putting the older geological formations on one copy of the map, the superficial accumulations and soils on another, the industrial information on a third, and so on. But without attempting to express all the detail possible, we may construct a correct and serviceable

D

geological map of a district or country by generalising
the information so as to give at a glance a broad and
clear view of the distribution of the formations and the
chief points of geological structure.

The Geological Survey of Great Britain and Ireland is
constructed chiefly upon field-maps (Ordnance Survey), on
the scale of six inches to the British statute mile, or
$\frac{1}{10560}$ of nature, but some limited districts, where great
detail is required, have been surveyed on the scale of
twenty-five inches to the mile. The general geological
map of the British Islands is published on the scale of
one inch to the mile, or $\frac{1}{63360}$ of nature. A convenient
scale for a generalised map of a country is ten miles to an
inch. Of course the smaller the scale the less detail is
possible, and the more care must be taken to select those
geological features which are of prime consequence.

More important than the scale is the correctness of the
topographical map which is to serve as the basis of the
geological one. Unless the geography be accurately
depicted, geological lines may be distorted, sometimes to
an extent which seriously interferes with the value of the
map. The importance of this point will be understood
from two diagrams (Fig. 3), which represent the influence
of correct and incorrect topography upon geological lines.
It will be observed that the same district is represented
in both drawings ; the streams and their tributaries are
the same in both, but differ considerably in direction. A
geologist trusting to the map A inserts the boundary lines
between the formations 1, 2, 3, 4, and 5, guiding himself
by the points of intersection of the different streams. If
now he were to trace these same lines on a map with the
correct topography, as shown in B, he would find them to

present considerable differences from those on A, although crossing each stream at the same points on each map. In A his thick black line is a winding one, in B it is

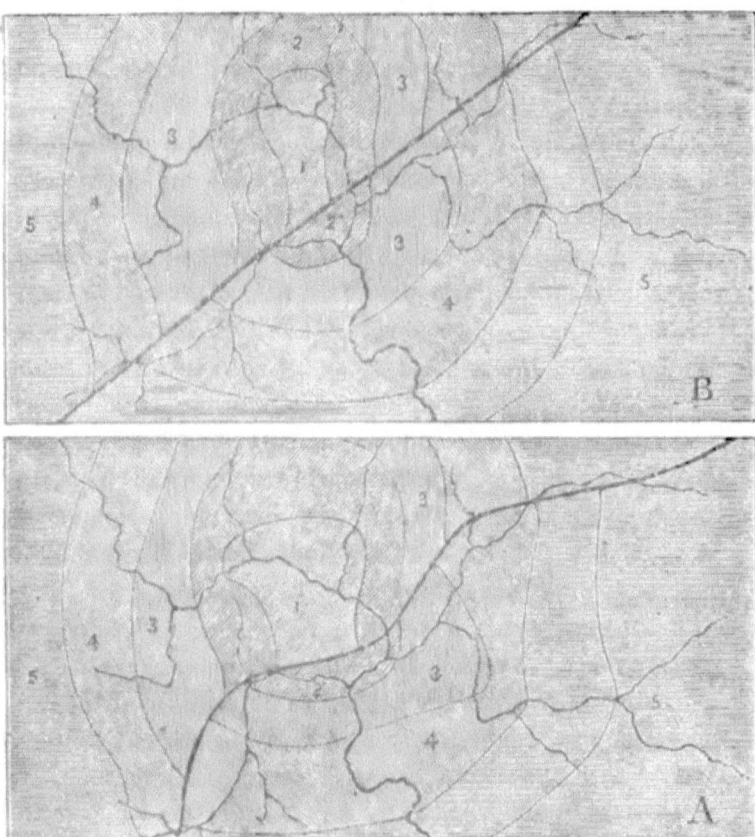

FIG. 3.—Maps showing the effect of incorrect topography in distorting geological lines.

nearly straight.   Should this boundary be a line of dislocation, the reader will see that by the one map he might be led to speculate upon a curved dislocation, in the other on a straight one.

In this country we fortunately possess accurate Ordnance maps on various scales, so that except in those few and remote districts of which the Ordnance Survey has not yet been completed, we have a good topographical basis, and may reach any degree of finish and completeness in geological map-making. It is useful, however, to be able to construct our own rough field-map, or to correct a faulty one. For this purpose we avail ourselves of the ordinary methods of triangulation. We may measure, as accurately as practicable, a base-line along some level piece of ground, such as a river-meadow or a sea-shore. From each end of our measured line we take a bearing with an azimuth compass to some neighbouring object. The point of intersection of the lines of these two bearings gives the position of the object on the map. Having one or two triangles constructed in this way, we may continue triangulating the whole district and filling in the topography, so as in the end to produce a map which may not be quite accurate indeed, but which will probably serve our immediate purpose.

In those parts of the world where no good maps yet exist, geological and topographical surveying are sometimes conjoined. I may cite, as admirable illustrations of this union, the explorations of the river-courses of Canada by the late Sir William Logan, Director of the Canadian Geological Survey. He and his colleagues had to furnish themselves with canoes, attendant Indians, provisions, and hunting-gear, and push up unexplored rivers, winding through the dense forests of the province. They explored, mapped, geologised, and hunted, laying down lines of traverse which served as the base for future more detailed topography, and did vast service in opening up the country. Still more elaborately topographical were the remarkable surveys lately carried out under Dr. Hayden, Geologist in charge of the Geological and Geographical Survey of the Western Territories of the United States. Year by year valuable reports, drawings, and photographs by that able observer and his associates made known the geography, geology, natural history, botany, meteorology, ethnology, and antiquities of thousands of square miles of previously unexplored or but partially explored land.

Having obtained or made as good a topographical map as may be attainable for his purpose, the observer is furnished with the first great requisite for geological surveying, and one of the most useful parts of the equipment of a field-geologist, whether he attempts any actual surveying or not.

Next to accuracy, judgment, and patience, neatness of hand is desirable in the geologist who would work out the structure of a district and express that structure on a map. Even the largest scale map does not admit of very voluminous notes upon its area, and where the scale is small there may be hardly room for notes of any kind. Under these circumstances the observer will do well to practise with the finest point to his pencil, making the neatest and most legible writing. After a brief experience he will find that he necessarily adopts a system of signs and contractions on his map, not only to save writing, but to prevent the map from being so overcrowded with notes as to become hopelessly confused. Every field-geologist insensibly invents contractions of his own. For the fundamental facts of geological structure, however, it is eminently desirable that the same

signs and symbols should be used with the same meaning
on all published geological maps.   The subjoined diagram shows some of the signs used on the maps of the
Geological Survey of Great Britain and Ireland.

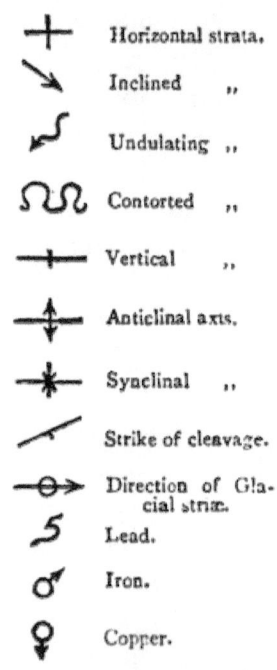

Horizontal strata.

Inclined   ,,

Undulating ,,

Contorted   ,,

Vertical   ,,

Anticlinal axis.

Synclinal   ,,

Strike of cleavage.

Direction of Gla-
    cial striæ.

Lead.

Iron.

Copper.

FIG. 4.—Some useful signs in geological surveying.

CHAPTER V.

HAVING now examined the various parts of the equipment of a field-geologist, let us proceed to notice what
use he must make of them. At the outset I would
remark that while the mere possession of good instruments cannot make a geologist, the want of them will
not prevent a skilled geologist from doing good work.
The training of years enables him to judge of rocks and
angles, of dip and of trends of boundary so nearly accurately as to make him often independent of hammer,
compass, and clinometer. In like manner long experience quickens his eye to detect geological evidence
where a less practised observer, though searching for
information, would fail to find it. This difference of
training tells greatly in all preliminary surveys, reconnaissances, or rapid traverses of a country. The geologist who has already had many years of campaigning
carries with him a faculty of grasping the salient features
of geological structure, and directing his attention, on
the march, to every available source of information which
will help him to fill in the details of his section. If it

were always practicable, the exploration of new regions, where the traveller is necessarily confined to his line of route, but where he has nevertheless to report on the geology of many thousands of square miles of territory, should be placed in the hands of men trained in geological surveying. That this arrangement would be of advantage will be, I think, admitted when we have entered a little more into the details of field-work.

No questions are probably put so frequently to the field-geologist as these—"How do you know what lies beneath the surface soil? Do you dig or bore?" When he replies that he neither digs nor bores, yet can usually infer with considerable confidence what must be the nature of the rock underneath, his statement is received with a look of bewilderment or a half-incredulous smile. But though the geologist does not usually dig or bore, he avails himself of every artificial opening he can hear of as offering any information with regard to the rocks beneath the surface. Every natural exposure of rock comes under his notice. If there is a coast-line, he makes a preliminary traverse of it, to ascertain the general nature of the rocks. He ascends one or more of the stream-courses for the same purpose. If there is any commanding hill in his district, he makes an early excursion to its top, that he may gain some general idea of the form of the ground and the probable distribution of the geological formations, so far as may be indicated by the landscape. On such occasions he will find the very great advantage of being able to sketch in his note-book an outline of the landscape. By so doing, he fixes the features in his mind in their natural proportions; he has the original sketch to refer to and to recall impressions which cannot be preserved by written words; and he has his attention drawn to those prominent features where probably he may meet with most interesting and profitable geological work. First jottings of this kind in a country never before visited, and of which the geological structure is still unknown to the observer, have for him a special interest and value. They retain for him the natural effect made on his eye and mind by the scenery, apart altogether from any explanation he may eventually be able to offer of the meaning of the features which he impartially sketches. With increasing experience of geological structure and practice in sketching it, these rapid drawings or notes gain in precision and fulness.

At first, of course, the observer may expect to find innumerable difficulties in his traverses of a country. He may find it impossible to take in any general conception of the whole region; everything seems lost perhaps in endless multiplicity of detail. But as he masters the detail, his power of grasping, at an early period in the examination of a district, the salient features of the geology, will steadily increase. In particular, he will be gratified to discover that he can, with growing success, identify rocks and formations even from a distance by their outlines, colour, character of vegetation, or other distinctive trait. His first surmises regarding the geological structure of the ground, made during his preliminary excursions, will thus come to be more and more sustained by his subsequent surveys. In later chapters it will be seen by what steps he may most profitably acquire this kind of experience.

The nature and conduct of these preliminary examinations not only vary with the character of the geology
and physical features of the country, they differ according to the extent to which the country is settled and
populous, or trackless and unexplored ; according to the
existence or absence of maps of the region to be examined ; according to climate and other obvious causes.
Such peculiarities as these, which greatly affect the first
general traverses of a country, are apt to influence all
the subsequent more detailed work.

As an illustration of the different conditions under
which field-geology may be carried on, let me contrast
the work of the Geological Survey of Great Britain and
Ireland with that of the United States Geological and
Geographical Survey of the Western Territories.   In
this long-settled and populous country we have abundant
means of communication by road, railway, or steamboat
between all or almost all districts.   Villages and towns
are scattered so numerously over the land that we seldom
need be in any doubt as to obtaining good quarters and
food.   The penny-post and electric telegraph accompany
us even into some of the most retired spots.   Books,
specimens, and instruments can be sent to us at a few
days' notice.   Of nearly every district in the British
Islands we may procure detailed Ordnance maps, by
which to make our way over the ground, and on which
to place the results of our geological observations.
Besides, the main features and much of the detail of
British geology are already known, and have been expressed with more or less precision upon published
geological maps.   We cannot, therefore, begin anywhere
in this small country without some kind of general know-

ledge about the formations and structure of the district
we may propose to examine.

There is still another element to be taken into account
as determining the character and methods of field-geology in Britain—one which perhaps geologists themselves
hardly sufficiently recognise—the climate of the country.
I do not believe that any one who has not daily occasion
to be out for many hours in the open air, and whose
avocations make him to some extent dependent upon
the weather, can have any proper notion of how good
the average weather of this country is, and how few
thoroughly bad days there are in the year when he
cannot secure even an hour or two of outdoor exercise.
Our summers are seldom too hot to prevent the full use
of a long July day. Our winters are so mild, and in
many seasons bring so little snow, that if need be we
may in most years carry on field-work up to the end
of December, and renew it at the beginning of January.

Such being the conditions under which field-geology
may be prosecuted in Britain, it is evident that an
observer may start for any district of the country alone
and investigate its structure by himself. There is no
occasion for combining a geological party, though that
may be done if need be. In the organised field-work of
the Geological Survey each officer has his own area
assigned to him, and works out its geology himself,
consulting, of course, from time to time his colleagues,
who may be stationed in adjoining tracts, and arranging
with them as to the joining-up of their various geological
boundary lines.

The extent of ground which can be examined and
mapped in a year by one of the geologists of the

Survey varies, not only with the capacity of the surveyor, but with the nature of the ground, whether level, easily traversed, and with comparatively few geological sections, or rough and high, laborious to climb or cross, and abounding in streams and crags, all of which must be examined and mapped. A man might complete the survey of half a county lying upon the chalk of the south-east of England before another could get over more than a part of a single parish in such intricate geological and rough mountainous ground as that round Snowdon, or that in many districts of Scotland.

Let me place before the reader some statistics respecting the rate of work in the Geological Survey of Scotland, where much of the ground is hilly and where the geological structure is often far from simple. The average annual area of ground geologically examined and surveyed by each officer in the field is not much below 100 square miles. This amount is performed by an average daily walk of from ten to fifteen miles, exclusive of Sundays, holidays, wet days, and the time spent indoors in reducing the field-work and preparing it for publication. The part of the year devoted to actual surveying may be set down as about 200 days, or it may be perhaps rather more than that. We see, then, that one of the members of the Scottish Geological Survey walks about 2,000 or 2,500 miles in the course of the year. Every square mile of his completed map represents, therefore, on the average, about twenty or twenty-five miles of actual walking.

It will be readily believed, that with all the advantages for field-geology in Britain it should be possible here to construct the most elaborate geological maps. I would refer to some of the published sheets of the Geological Survey of the United Kingdom for an illustration of what can be, and has been, done in this respect. I do not suppose that any such detailed geological work has been elsewhere attempted. The large maps on the scale of six inches to the mile, with which the field-work is now chiefly conducted, admit of almost unlimited detail. Every important or interesting stratum may be put down and traced on these maps; little dislocations of only a few feet in extent may be shown even when they are pretty closely crowded together; no feature of geological value need be omitted for want of space to express it. As illustrations of intricate and detailed geological mapping I may cite sheets 14, 15, 22, and 23 of the one-inch Geological Survey Map of Scotland, and the corresponding six-inch coal-field maps belonging to the same tract of the country.

Now with field-geology and map-making as possible, and as actually accomplished, in Britain, let us contrast the conditions under which work of this kind must be carried on in an unexplored region like the Western Territories of the United States. The survey of vast tracts in those parts of the North American continent by Hayden, King, and Powell proves them to be among the most zealous, active, and efficient geologists who ever undertook the task of pioneering through a new country. But the utmost skill and experience cannot alter the natural features of a country and its climate. The American survey requires to be carried on in a very different manner from ours, and I cite it as an excellent example of how field-geology can be prosecuted in new and previously unmapped regions.

As the topographical map of the country required to be made, Dr. Hayden's survey was at once geographical and geological. His staff contained more topographers than geologists. It required division into separate working parties, to each of which a distinct tract of country was assigned. From the higher hill-tops triangulations were made and outline-sketches were taken, so that a general map was traced and filled in. In this work the geologists co-operated, indicating to their associates the salient geological features of each region, and inserting these upon sections or diagrams, which, for beauty and effectiveness, are among the most remarkable geological sketches which have yet been produced.

Besides the scientific staff, however, provision had to be made for a foraging department; and sometimes, also, an escort has been needed, where the work lay in or near the territories of hostile Indians.

As a sample of the equipment of Dr. Hayden's survey I may cite a few particulars from his Report for 1874. The staff in the field was divided into seven parties. Of the organisation of these, the first may be taken as a type. It consisted of one assistant geologist as director, two topographers, two meteorologists, one botanist and collector, one general assistant, two packers, cook, and hunter. It would seem that there was thus only one geologist in the party, though probably one or two of the other members were able to lend him some assistance. Starting on the 20th of July, the party continued the campaign till the 27th of November. During that time it surveyed 4,300 square miles of new ground, which is probably an average of somewhere about forty square miles a day. This working party, therefore, though probably not much more than one geologist strong, accomplished in three days as great an area of work as one of my colleagues finds it possible to complete in a year. Such rapid surveying can of course be regarded as furnishing merely a kind of rough preliminary sketch of the geology of the territories, to serve as the basis for future detailed surveys. It may be taken as an example of broad generalised field-work on the one hand, while the Geological Survey of Britain stands at the opposite extreme, as a model of patient and elaborate detail.

The student may usefully refer to other examples of such pioneering geological exploration in Western America. Of these, the "Exploration of the Fortieth Parallel," under Mr. Clarence King, and the "Geological and Geographical Survey of the Rocky Mountain Region," under Major Powell, well deserve perusal. The more recent monographs of Captain Dutton, of the United States Geological Survey, may also be profitably studied.

CHAPTER VI.

WHETHER field-geology is to be carried on rapidly and in a generalised way, or slowly and in detail, the same methods must be followed. I have supposed the geologist to have selected and reached his ground, and to have made a few preliminary traverses to gain some notion of the chief rocks and their arrangement. Let us follow his subsequent operations.

The brooks, ravines, sea-coasts, hill-sides, valleys, and mountains, in short every natural section or artificial exposure of the rocks, will be carefully examined, and the observations made will be registered in note-book or map at the time. In the course of these rambles three points will have to be settled : first, the lithology and distribution of the rocks; second, their probable or actual geological horizon or date ; third, their position with regard to each other, that is, the geological structure of the district.

The determination of the nature of the rocks is obviously the first question which must be dealt with. And here it must be remembered that the term rock is applied in geology indifferently to all kinds of naturally-formed stones which occur in mass, even to peat, blown sand, and mud. Taking them in this wide sense, the geologist considers, with regard to those he encounters in the field, whether they are Fragmental, Derivative, or Stratified (*Klastische Gesteine*), and, if so, whether they are conglomerates, sandstones, shales, clays, limestones, ironstones, or other varieties of this great series ; whether, on the other hand, they are Crystalline or Igneous rocks, and if so, whether they should be classed as granite, syenite, diorite, basalt, gabbro, serpentine, or other species of this family ; or whether they are to be called Foliated or Metamorphic rocks, such as gneiss, mica-schist, or hornblende-slate. To be able to answer these questions, the observer must have trained his eye by the examination of good typical specimens of rocks. This is a kind of knowledge not to be obtained from books ; it can only be gathered from patient and intelligent handling of the rocks themselves. In the field the observer who has had this training in PETROGRAPHY, as the study of rocks is termed, can usually recognise the rocks he encounters. A pocket knife, lens, and acid-bottle will assist him if his eye does not readily detect the characters of the stone. But it will often happen that he requires to subject a rock to more careful examination at home, before he can decide as to its nature and name.

It is absolutely necessary, however, that the field-geologist should have already familiarised his eye with certain important minerals which enter largely into the composition of rocks, so as to be able to identify and distinguish them, and thereby the rocks which they constitute. For this purpose he should procure a collection of these minerals, and subject them to careful examina-

E.

tion, so as to fix their characters in his mind; while at
the same time he will not omit to devote as much time
as he can spare to the attentive study of any good
mineralogical cabinet within his reach.   The number of
minerals which form essential constituents of widely-
diffused rocks is comparatively small.   Nor are those
very numerous which occur abundantly as accessory
or accidental ingredients.   In Chapter XVI. the reader
will find a list of those which it is desirable that he
should know, with a reference to the part they play as
constituents of rocks.

But if the geologist means to devote himself to the
study of the genesis of rocks, particularly those of
igneous and metamorphic origin, he will find it needful to
enter much more fully into the domain of MINERALOGY.
Nor will he regret such an excursion; for in studying
the structure and growth of minerals he learns how rocks
have been formed, and by what processes they have been
altered since their formation.   This is well brought out
by the microscopical examination of crystals, as will be
pointed out in a later chapter.

Though practice alone can give the learner justifiable
confidence among rocks in the field, some hints may be
offered here for his guidance.   He must learn to distinguish between essential and accidental characters.   Two
rocks for instance may exactly resemble each other in
colour, and even in shade of colour, yet the one may be
a derivative or sedimentary mass, the other an original
or igneous one.   Colour, therefore, can hardly be a very
trustworthy index of the true nature of a rock.   Again, a
rock may at one place be so compact and tough as to be
broken with difficulty, though at a short distance it may

be as soft as loose gravel or sand. Wide variations in texture likewise occur; a mass of rock will here present a coarsely crystalline or almost granitoid aspect, while there it may be so close-grained as to appear nearly homogeneous.

In his field-work, therefore, the learner will discover by experience what are the essential characters in each case. Reserving more precise and detailed investigation for indoor-work (see Chap. XVI.), he will find that with the unaided eye and such instruments as can be carried in the field, he can take note of the following particulars of the rocks: 1. Fresh fracture and weathered surface. 2. Structure and texture. 3. Hardness and streak. 4. Colour. 5. Smell. 6. Feel. 7. Behaviour in mass.

I. Fresh Fracture and Weathered Surface. —All rocks yield more or less to the corroding action of the atmosphere. Some, like pure limestone, are merely dissolved by rain, and remain with a bare, clean, hard surface. But most of them show a more or less distinct

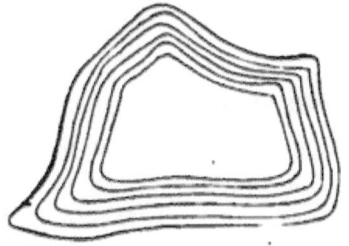

Fig. 5.—Weathered crust, showing concentric zones of oxidation.

crust or outer crumbling skin, which is thicker or thinner, according to the resisting power of the rock on the one hand, and the vigour of the decomposing agents on the other. In this outer weathered crust we may often observe the composition of the rock better than on the fresh fracture. The very existence of such a crust depends upon unequal decay; some one or more ingredients of the rock disappear faster than the others, which may remain isolated and comparatively little altered in the crumbling *débris* of the decomposed constituent. For example, in many close-grained and crystalline rocks, consisting of quartz and felspar, these two minerals are so intermingled and so resemble each other in colour and lustre, that at a first glance they might not be distinguished; but on a weathered surface their clearly defined differences stand out very sharply; the felspar has a dull earthy texture and white colour, while the quartz projects in hard glassy grains. A large number of rocks are characterised each by its own type of weathering. Thus, granite is apt to split along its joints and to assume, as it decays, the aspect of ruined walls and buttresses of cyclopean masonry. Basalt rocks are prone to develop a spheroidal structure, each globular mass exfoliating into concentric onion-like coats (Fig. 6). Limestone projects in bare, smooth, bleached knobs, curiously fretted, channelled, and honeycombed; the grass around is usually greener than elsewhere, and the ground is often perforated with swallow-holes, tunnels, and ramifying passages.

The contrast between a weathered and a fresh piece of the same rock is often so extreme that the beginner would not willingly admit them to be from the same mass, unless he had himself detached them. Basalt, for instance, on a fresh unaltered fracture, is a compact or finely crystalline rock, heavy, and of an iron-black colour. But on a weathered cliff it may be seen of every hue from bright yellow to sombre brown, and in many places so soft as to be capable of being dug out with a spade. The beginner, therefore, should on no

FIG. 6.—Dolerite (basalt) weathering spheroidally.   North Queensferry.

account omit to make himself acquainted both with the unaltered and the altered conditions of rocks. By degrees he will learn to recognise a rock through all its protean disguises of weathering, and distinguish it even at some distance.

II. Structure and Texture.—The nature of the component particles, and the manner in which they are arranged so as to build up the mass of the rock, constitute important characters. The geologist in the field has of course only very limited means of investigating these characters, so that when they become doubtful and obscure he may be compelled to defer the solution of his difficulties until he can find opportunity in-doors of subjecting the rocks to more detailed and careful scrutiny. But with the aid of his pocket-lens he can recognise three types of structure among rocks which may be termed respectively Crystalline, Compact, and Fragmental.

i. CRYSTALLINE.—In this type the rocks have a granular structure, and on inspection the apparent grains are found to be crystals, or crystalline particles, so intermingled, or felted together, as to give coherence to the stone. In the coarse-grained varieties, like many granites, the crystals of which can be distinctly seen at a distance of several yards, their true crystalline nature is at once apparent. We see that their grains are all crystalline, and that the lustre reflected from so many shining points on their surface comes from the cleavage planes of the component minerals. But as the texture becomes finer, as it does, for example, in the family of the basalt rocks, the unassisted eye may hardly be able to detect any crystalline facettes, even on a fresh fracture. The lens, however, will often show that such rocks really consist of very small crystals. But the fineness of grain may reach such a point as to escape detection even by that means, and then the observer must call the rock a compact one. It may still be quite crystalline, however, when examined under the microscope, in the manner described in a later chapter. We are at present concerned only with those external characters which can be recognised by the observer in the field.

The crystalline particles are found to be built up on two different plans. In the great majority of rocks they are (i) amorphously aggregated, that is, they have crystallized together promiscuously without any definite arrangement, so that the rock presents much the same

FIG. 7.—A piece of granite. Crystalline structure.

texture no matter in what direction it may be broken; (ii) schistose or foliated, that is, disposed in more or less distinctly parallel folia or laminæ.

(1st) Amorphously aggregated.—Rocks of this kind are a, *Simple*, or β, *Compound*.

(a) *Simple*.—Composed essentially of one mineral, though now and then with accessory ingredients. The rocks of this sub-group are almost entirely of aqueous origin, that is, they have crystallized from solutions in water. Crystalline limestone, gypsum, and rock-salt may be taken as illustrative examples. A few silicates occur in this form, as hornblende-rock, but most of them incline to the foliated type.

(β) *Compound.*—Composed of two or more minerals in an infinite variety of proportions. Most of the rocks which constitute this very important series are what are usually called Igneous ; that is, they have crystallized out of molten solutions like modern lava. They almost invariably consist of silicates of alumina, with magnesia, lime, potass, soda, and varying proportions of iron oxides, phosphate of lime, &c. The great majority of them are mainly composed of some felspar, or at least contain a large percentage of that mineral, with such silicates as hornblende, augite, olivine, biotite, and muscovite ; free silica in the form of blebs or crystals of quartz ; iron oxides, particularly magnetic and titaniferous ; apatite, &c. Hence they are commonly distinguishable from the simple rocks by their greater hardness, toughness, and weight. Granite, syenite, quartz-porphyry, basalt, diorite, are examples of compound rocks.

Many varieties of texture occur among these rocks. The following are among the more important :—*Coarse-crystalline : fine-crystalline ; (crypto-crystalline*, where the

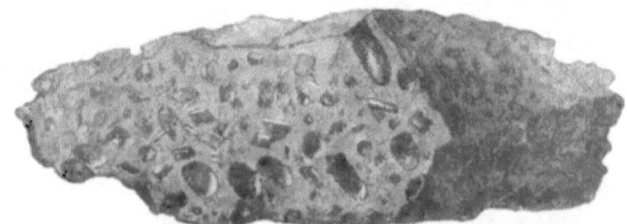

FIG. 8.—Piece of lava, showing crystals and steam-holes.

crystals are so minute as to appear only under the microscope, might be placed by the field-geologist among the compact series) ; *porphyritic*—having large

crystals, usually of felspar, scattered through a compact
base; *cellular*—full of spherical cavities formed by the
expansion of imprisoned steam during the outflow of the
rock (Fig. 8); *scoriaceous*—roughly and irregularly cellular, like the scoriæ of a lava stream, or the "clinkers"
from a foundry; *amygdaloidal*—full of almond-shaped
concretions of calcite, calcedony, zeolites, or other minerals; these concretions having been deposited by infil-
tration in steam-holes of the rock, so that when they
weather out, the original cellular aspect of the mass is
restored.

(2nd) S c h i s t o s e.—Rocks of this group are readily
distinguishable by the peculiar arrangement of their
component minerals into parallel layers or folia. These
layers consist sometimes of one mineral, as in horn-
blende-schist; more usually they are composed of two
or more minerals, as in mica-schist and gneiss. They
may be observed to run into each other and to be as it
were welded together. Yet they are distinctly crystalline. In many cases they present a wrinkled or crumpled
aspect, as if they had been puckered up by strong lateral
pressure.

ii. COMPACT.—Without recognizable component crystals
or particles, so far as can be made out in the field, but
with a close, homogeneous texture. Three leading
varieties may be noticed—1st, Glassy; 2nd, Horny; 3rd,
Fine-grained.

(1st) G l a s s y—resembling bottle-glass or pitch. This
sub-group includes the natural glasses, as obsidian, and
pitchstone. Some hydrocarbons, as asphalt and anthracite, might be included here.

(2nd) H o r n y—having a feebly lustrous, translucent

character, like flint. The chalk-flints and the cherts of older formations are good examples.

(3rd) F i ne-g r a i n e d—having a dull, exceedingly close granular texture, which may pass into the fine varieties of the crystalline amorphous rocks on the one hand, and of the fragmental rocks on the other. Many limestones and felsites show this texture. Hence, as it characterises rocks of very different geological structure and origin, it evidently must be used with caution as a means of identifying them. Other characters should be looked for, and perhaps in the end appeal must be made to the microscope.

iii. FRAGMENTAL (*Clastic*)—composed of fragments of pre-existing rocks or minerals. As rocks of this type are mere mechanical mixtures, they present endless variety, both in composition and texture. In the vast

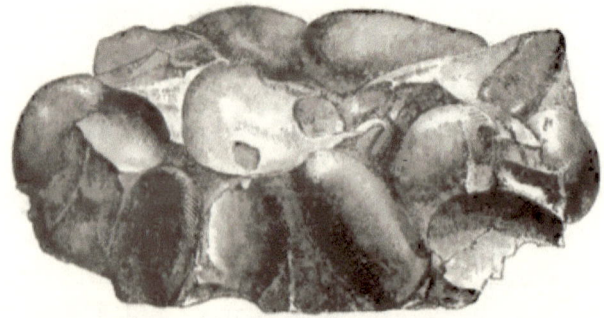

FIG. 9.—Piece of conglomerate, showing the characteristic rounded water-worn aspect of the component parts of many fragmental rocks.

majority of cases they are of aqueous origin, that is, they have been laid down as sediment in water. Their component grains are therefore usually more or less rounded and water-worn (Fig. 9), even when consisting of crystal-

line particles derived from older rocks.   The coarse
varieties, consisting of compacted gravel, are termed
conglomerates when formed of rounded, *breccias* when
formed of angular fragments.   These coarse-grained
rocks pass into *grits* and *sandstones*, where the materials, usually more or less siliceous, have been
ground down into sand.   *Argillaceous* rocks are those
composed of the finer or clayey sediment, sometimes
arranged in laminæ of deposit, as in *shale*, at other
times with no fissility, as in *fireclay* and *mud*.   An important series of fragmental rocks has been formed by
the consolidation of the loose dust and blocks ejected
by a volcano.   To these the general term *Tuffs* has
been applied.   (Fig. 10.)

FIG. 10.—Piece of volcanic tuff.

With the fragmental rocks may be classed those
which have been formed of the fragmentary remains of
plants and animals.   Ordinary crinoidal limestone is a
characteristic example, consisting as it does of the con-
gregated joints and plates of encrinites, with more or
less perfect mollusca, corals, echini, fish-teeth, &c.
Some of these organically derived rocks, however, possess textures which would justify their being called

compact rocks, as in the case of cannel coal. Others, again, have acquired, in large measure, a crystalline texture, as has happened so abundantly in the Mountain Limestone. The reader is referred to Chapters XVI. and XVII. for further information on this subject.

FIG. 11.—P.ece of coal, composed of matted stems of *Sigillaria* and *Lepidodendron.* Carmarthenshire. (De la Beche.)

III. Hardness and Streak.—Rocks differ much from each other in hardness; even in the same mass of rock considerable diversities in this respect may be met with. Hardness is a character of secondary importance, though it may often be usefully employed to distinguish, among the compact rocks, siliceous from softer calcareous masses. Obviously it can only be properly applied to perfectly fresh surfaces, and is suited to homogeneous rather than to compound rocks. The scale of hardness employed in mineralogy may be used in testing rocks.

1. Talc.	6. Orthoclase.
2. Rock-salt.	7. Quartz.
3. Calcite.	8. Topaz.
4. Fluor spar.	9. Corundum (Emery).
5. Apatite.	10. Diamond.

A rock which can be easily scratched with the finger-nail, like many chloritic-schists, may be said to have one degree of hardness, or H 1; rocks possessing the hardness of rock-salt (2) can be less easily scratched with the finger-nail. The pocket-knife easily marks a limestone or crystal of calcite (3), which, on the other hand, resists the finger-nail; a little more pressure is required to mark a crystal of fluor-spar (4), and still more one of apatite (5). Rocks possessing the sixth degree of hardness can be scratched with the knife with difficulty, while when they possess greater hardness than about $6\frac{1}{2}$ degrees they resist the knife and even turn its edge, or take a streak of steel. Hence as rocks of this resisting power are almost always siliceous, the application of the knife furnishes a convenient means of discriminating them.

Streak is the name given to the powder made when the knife (or file, or diamond) is drawn across the surface of a mineral or rock. Though sometimes useful in mineralogy, it is not often of much service among rocks. It may now and then be employed to distinguish compact dark bituminous clays or shales from varieties of coal, the former giving a dull brown or grey powder, and the latter a lustrous black streak. In the case of impure calcareous rocks, when little or no effervescence is visible in a drop of weak acid placed upon the clean surface, brisk disengagement of carbonic acid may often be produced by dropping the acid over the powder made by a scratch with the knife. Of course, individual minerals which occur either as original or accidental constituents of rocks may be tried for streak in the usual way required in mineralogical inquiry. Small specks of hæmatite may thus be detected by their characteristic cherry-red streak, while the iron-peroxide when hydrated will show its brown or yellow streak.

IV. Colour.—Great caution must be exercised in making use of this character in the discrimination of rocks. The same rock may, even within short distances, display the most extraordinary varieties of colour. But within certain limits the colour of a rock is an indication of the nature of some at least of its constituents. Iron is the great pigment to which the rocks owe their diversities of hue. It gives rise to numerous tints of yellow, brown, red, and green, as well as to blue and black. Some hints as to the causes of a few common varieties of colour may be of service.

White.—Limestones and clays are often quite white, and in this condition are almost always at their purest. Iron is generally absent, or present in but small quantity, in white rocks. The result of weathering is often to bleach rocks white, the air and rain removing the colouring materials, more especially the iron. The stones in a morass, or below peat turf, are commonly bleached as white as chalk on the outside—the result of the reducing action of the organic matter on the iron oxides which are removed in solution as organic compounds or as carbonates.

Black.—Many carbonaceous rocks are black. Coals may be distinguished by their lightness, texture, and combustion. Clays or shales, rendered black by the

vegetable matter they contain, may be recognised by
their weight, streak, and their turning white but retaining
their shape when strongly heated. But black heavy rocks
abound in which there is no trace of carbon. These
very generally contain a considerable amount of iron,
either in the form of magnetite, ilmenite, or other related
oxide, or in that of some black ferruginous mineral, such
as hornblende. Such rocks are apt to weather with a
brown or yellow crust, owing to the conversion of the
iron into the hydrous peroxide.

Brown.—This colour characterises some rocks on their
fresh fractures, as the variety of ironstone called black-
band. A few crystalline rocks have a brown tint from
the presence of minerals of that colour, such as varieties
of mica and garnet. But it is more particularly on the
decomposed surfaces and crusts of rocks that brown tints
appear. The iron is there converted into the hydrous
peroxide, limonite. Basalt rocks show this change in a
most instructive manner. Earthy manganese also gives
dark brown to black tints.

Yellow.—The colouring material of yellow rocks is
almost always limonite. Yellow sandstones, beds of
ochre, the weathered crusts of many limestones and of
numerous ferruginous crystalline rocks furnish illustrations. Sometimes a metallic or brassy yellow is
communicated to parts of rocks by diffused iron-pyrites ;
when this yellow is of the pale kind due to marcasite, it
can only be seen on fresh fractures, as it disappears with
the rapid decomposition of the mineral.

Red.—The prevailing hue of red rocks varies from a
brownish-red to a bright brick-red, and is due to the
presence of the peroxide of iron, hæmatite. Such rocks

are often mottled with or pass into yellow and brown tints, where the iron they contain has been hydrated. These colours are most typically displayed among red sandstones and clays, of which an enormous mass occurs in the Old Red and New Red Sandstone, and in the Trias. Some rocks show a delicate flesh-red tint from the colour of their orthoclase felspar, as in pink granite. Iron is in this case also the pigment.

Green.—Many red sandstones are marked with circular spots of green, due to the reduction of the iron oxide. Protosilicate of iron is the prevalent green pigment of rocks; carbonates of copper sometimes colour rocks of bright verdigris and emerald green tints. Many magnesian silicates are green, and impart green colours of various hues to the rocks of which they are constituents. Thus hornblende and augite give rise to dark bottle-green, and among the schistose rocks to paler apple-green and leek-green tints. The hydrous forms of these silicates, talc, chlorite, and serpentine, form characteristically green rocks, the talc rocks shading off into white, and serpentine into black and dark red. Glauconite extensively diffused through certain sandstones gives them a characteristic green colour.

Blue is not a frequent colour in rock masses. It is often spoken of as the colour of many limestones, which, however, are grey or bluish-grey. Beautiful belts of pale blue and white occur among the schistose rocks where the mineral kyanite abounds. Some clays and lithomarges are of a pale lavender-blue. Patches of a bright smalt blue, or of an indigo tint, may be met with among peat-mosses, where some animal organism has decayed and given rise to the formation of phosphate of iron.

Grey may be said to be the prevailing colour among rocks, especially of the older geological periods. In simple rocks like limestones it is often produced by the intermingling of minute particles of clay, sand, or iron-oxide, or of amorphous carbonate of lime with the paler crystalline calcite of the comminuted organisms. Pure crystalline limestone is naturally snow-white, as in Carrara marble. In compound rocks the prevailing grey hues depend on the mixture of a white mineral, usually a felspar, with one or more dark minerals like magnetite, hornblende, or augite, the lightness or darkness of the hue depending upon the relative proportions of the constituents. Should the felspar be coloured by iron, a pinkish hue may be given to the grey; or if the dark magnesian silicates have been altered into some of their hydrous representatives, the grey becomes more or less distinctly green. The old "greenstones" owe their distinctive hue to this source.

V. Smell.—Clay-rocks may be recognised by the peculiar earthy odour they give out when breathed upon. Crystalline felspar rocks when breathed upon often yield this smell. Some rocks, especially limestones containing animal matter or decomposing iron sulphides, yield a fetid or rotten-egg smell when freshly broken.

VI. Feel.—A few rocks are characterised by a peculiar feeling to the touch. This is chiefly shown by the hydrous magnesian silicates, talc, chlorite, serpentine, &c. (also by some micaceous schists), which have a greasy or soapy feel. In large tracts of country formed of chlorite-schist, margarodite-schist, or serpentine rock, the stones have everywhere this characteristic. The term "trachyte" was originally applied

F

FIG. 12.—Outlines of mountains formed of stratified or sedimentary rocks.   Rocky Mountains.
(Hayden's Report of Survey of Western Territories, 1876.)

to certain volcanic rocks distinguished by the harsh,
prickly feeling experienced when the finger is passed
over their surface. A rock like chalk is said to be
meagre to the touch.

VII. Behaviour in Mass.—There are some remarkably characteristic aspects of rocks which cannot
be judged of in hand-specimens, any more than the
architecture of a building can be told from the nature
of the stone employed in its construction. It is as parts
of the architecture of the earth's crust that rocks present
many of their most typical and individual features.
These broader and larger characters show themselves in
the outline of every hill and mountain. As illustrations
we may take the two contrasted groups of the stratified
fragmental and amorphous crystalline rocks. Even from
a distance the difference between these rocks makes
itself felt in the striking distinctions so often visible in
the form of mountains. Thus in Fig. 12 it will be
noticed that two prominent sets of lines can be traced all
along the crests and declivities—the horizontal lines of
the bedding and the vertical lines of the joints. The
rocks are cut into huge blocks in the process of denudation, and these blocks are further channelled and chiselled
along the dominant divisional lines. With this recti-
linear style of architecture compare that of a mass of
granite, one of the amorphous crystalline rocks. No
parallel systems of lines here catch the eye. The
crests are splintered, indeed, along the joints, and these
divisional lines may be traced by a practised eye down
many of the cliffs and steep declivities of granite, but
they never show the definiteness, regularity, and alternation of prominent and retiring bands so typical of

F 2

FIG. 13.—Outlines of a mountain formed of crystalline rock.   Rocky Mountains.   (*Hayden's Report for 1874.*)

stratified rocks. The general lines of the mountain are graceful curves rising more and more towards the summits till they often become vertical.

The stratified rocks, then, are distinguished by their arrangement into beds, varying according to the nature of the substance, from the finest laminæ up to large masses many yards in thickness. The amorphous crystalline rocks, on the other hand, are marked by the absence of all structure except their joints. The reader will find this subject further illustrated in succeeding chapters; but he will learn more by a little practice in the field than can be easily communicated by books.

CHAPTER VII.

THE NATURE AND USE OF FOSSILS.

In probably the great majority of cases, it is the interest attaching to the remains of once living plants and animals imbedded in the rocks which induces people to read geological books and to devote their time to the endeavour to gain some practical acquaintance with geology. But as a rule the practical work begins and ends with the gathering of the specimens. In the present chapter I wish to show that apart from their interest or beauty as specimens which can be arranged in a collection, the relics of former organisms are of the utmost value in geological inquiry,—that in fact, so far as relates to the chronological succession of geological history, their importance is paramount.

A "fossil" is literally anything dug up. The word, formerly applied indiscriminately to any mineral substance taken out of the earth, whether possessing organized structure or not, is now restricted to the remains or traces of plants and animals which have been imbedded by natural causes in any geological formation, whether ancient rock or modern superficial deposit. Thus under the designation "fossil," we must include the entire

carcases of mammoths and rhinoceroses which have been
preserved for ages with their flesh and hair, frozen up in
some of the muddy soils of Siberia ; the skeleton of a
stag preserved in a peat-bog ; the scales and teeth of
fishes scattered through a solid limestone ; the shells of
mollusca, the calcareous framework of corals, the compressed leaves, fruits, and stems of plants; in short, any
and every part of an organism which has been imbedded
in a geological formation, no matter what may be its
condition of preservation, and whether or not it has been
partially or wholly petrified.

But not merely must we include every portion of the
organism ; we may properly class also with fossils every
substance or marking which has been connected in any
way with the organism and bears witness as to its existence and character. Thus, the resin of a tree, the trail
or the castings of a worm, the droppings of animals,
even the tools and weapons of man, may all become
fossils and yield their evidence as to former conditions of
life.

As the circumstances under which fossils have been
entombed have greatly varied, the observer must be prepared for the most extraordinary differences in the appearance of even the same species of fossil in different places
and kinds of rock. In some rare examples the body of
the animal has been so entirely and perfectly preserved
that its flesh when first disinterred may actually be eaten,
as was the case with the Siberian mammoth just referred
to, which was so fresh as to be torn in pieces and devoured
by beasts and birds of prey. As a rule, however, the
soft parts of the organism are gone. Where there have
been harder parts, such as an internal skeleton or an

external covering, these may still remain nearly or quite
in their original condition.   As a rule, however, even the
harder parts have undergone some change ; they have
lost some portions of their original substance, more
particularly the animal matter, and have had mineral
material infiltrated instead.   And the process of replace-
ment has often continued until every particle of the
original bone or shell or stem has been removed and
has been replaced by carbonate of lime, silica, spathic
iron, or some other mineral whereby the minute structure
of the organism has been perfectly preserved.   In other
cases the whole of the animal or plant has disappeared,
and has been replaced by a cast which retains the external
form of the original, but is internally entirely structureless ;
or the cast, if there ever was one, has been destroyed,
and only an empty cavity remains to mark where the
organism once lay.   In the case of the mollusca we may
have either a cast of the external or internal form of the
shell.   The observer will often be puzzled at first by
such internal casts, as he will at once understand if he
takes the two valves of an empty oyster-shell, places them
in their original position, and, after making a small hole
in one of them, pours in liquid plaster of Paris until the
internal cavity is filled with it.   When the plaster has
set he can remove the valves, and he will have an internal cast of the oyster.   But had he seen the object
before making the experiment, he would not have been
likely to guess what it was.

Again, at the outset he may experience some difficulty
in identifying the same fossil when it occurs in different·
kinds of stone.   For example, a plant which, when preserved in shale or any argillaceous layer, may retain each

leaflet, scar, and surface-marking, will perhaps appear in sandstone as a mere black streak of coaly substance. A fossil fish, which if found in a limestone nodule may have every scale and bone in place, each with its peculiar sculpture delicately shown, may, if met with in a conglomerate, occur merely in scattered fragments, all so much rounded and worn as to be hardly recognisable.

A little experience will guide the learner to those rocks which are likely to contain fossils. No general rule can be laid down; for the kinds of rock which are barren of organic remains in some places, abound with them in others. Conglomerates, for example, are not usually rocks in which we should expect to meet with fossils; nor as a rule do we find them there. Yet there are many richly fossiliferous conglomerates, such as those of the Silurian rocks of Penwhapple Glen in Ayrshire, and of the Upper Old Red Sandstone in several parts of Scotland. Argillaceous rocks are commonly better grounds for fossil-hunting than sandstones, and limestones are better than either. The shaly bands however which lie above a limestone are often more prolific than the limestone itself, as the fossils can be extracted entire from the soft, surrounding matrix.

The inspection of a well-arranged series of fossils in a museum, all cleaned and neatly labelled, affords but small assistance in the practical work of finding the fossils in the rocks. The learner must betake himself to the localities from which he knows that fossils have already been obtained; or if it is a district not yet explored for fossils, he must carefully note first of all the characters of the rocks. He will discover after some practice that it is not luck, but skill and good eyesight, which make

the successful collector. Two observers may go over
the same ground; one of them diligently applies his
hammer, breaks up innumerable blocks of limestone,
finds not a single recognisable trace of a fossil, and
pronouncing the rock to be unfossiliferous, passes on; the
other, perceiving the calcareous nature of the stone,
and therefore its possibly fossiliferous character, puts his
hammer in his belt, and betakes himself at once to the

FIG. 14.—Fossils standing in relief on a weathered surface of limestone.

weathered blocks. He knows, as every one soon does who
attends to the subject, that in many cases a rock, which
is really highly fossiliferous, may not appear to be so on a
fresh fracture, where the whole texture of the stone may
be uniformly crystalline. But when exposed to the slow
corrosive influence of the weather, the difference between
the molecular arrangement of the calcareous matter in the

organic remains and in the surrounding matrix begins to appear. Shells, corals, and crinoids stand out in relief on the weathered stone, showing even some of their most delicate sculpturing, while the surrounding limestone has been slowly dissolved and removed. In this way a rock which may have been supposed to be unfossiliferous by one observer is shown by another of greater training to be full of fossils. Old walls and buildings, the refuse heaps of old quarries, the angular blocks strewn at the base of a cliff—in short, all surfaces of rock which have been lying exposed for a long while to the gentle influences of the air, rain, and frosts, may be made to yield their evidence as to the fossils in the rocks of a district.

There are five important purposes to which the geologist can apply the fossils he may encounter among the rocks : first, to throw light upon revolutions in climate ; second, to restore former conditions of geography ; third, to detect former movements in the crust of the earth ; fourth, to afford horizons which serve to unravel geological structure ; and fifth, to fix the relative geological date of rocks.

1. *Climate.*—Within certain limits, fossils may be employed to show under what conditions of climate the geological formations of bygone ages were accumulated. We know, for example, that in the older tertiary periods in Europe the temperature must have been considerably higher than it is now, for in strata of that age we find among the fossil plants, forms of palm, custard-apple, laurel, fig, and numerous conifers ; together with remains of turtles, crocodiles, sea-snakes, tapir-like pachyderms, and many mollusca belonging to genera now living in warmer seas than those of Western and North-

western Europe.   On the other hand, it can be shown
that the general climate of Central and Northern Europe
at a later time became quite arctic in character, for the
remains of the reindeer and the musk-ox occur in
superficial formations even far south in France ; bones
of the arctic lemming, mammoth, woolly rhinoceros,
and other northern mammalia, mark the cave-deposits
and other surface accumulations in the South of England ;
shells now extinct in our littoral waters, but still living in
those of northern seas, abound in the clays which fringe
the coasts of the West of Scotland.

It must be borne in mind, however, that the argument
from organic remains may be pushed too far.   When we
are dealing with species no longer living, we need an
accumulation of evidence to warrant any deduction from
them as to climate.   Two species of the same genus may
flourish under very different conditions of climate, as we
may see from the fact that the Elephas primigenius or
mammoth was a thick-furred northern form, though
his modern representatives inhabit intertropical latitudes.
Hence it is not by one species, but by the whole assemblage of the plants and animals, or what is called the
fossil flora and fauna, of a formation, that the climate in
which the organisms lived must be judged.   The further
removed the fossils are from us in time, the more do
they differ from living forms, and the less reliable are
they as witnesses to climate.

2. *Geographical Conditions.*—In most cases it is only
from the character of the included organic remains that
the conditions under which stratified deposits were laid
down can be determined.   By the evidence of fossils
we may confidently identify former land-surfaces, lake-

bottoms, and sea-bottoms. (1) Land-surfaces are revealed to us by layers of terrestrial vegetation resting upon what must once have been soil, and which still contains the roots of the plants that grew upon it. Stumps of trees in their position of growth, with, it may be, their fruits and leaves lying around, and even an occasional wing-case of a beetle, or the remains of a lizard or land-snail, furnish unimpeachable proof that the localities where they occur were once tree-covered tracts of ground. Hence the occurrence of such a

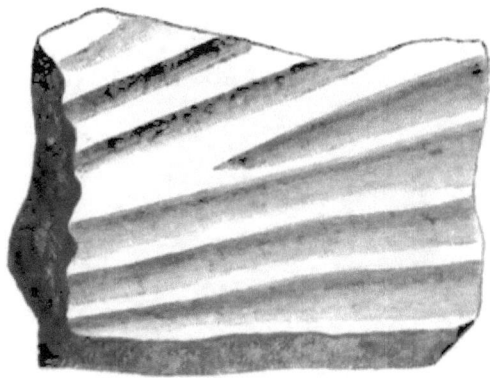

Fig. 15.—Ripple marks in sandstone.

terrestrial layer in a group of strata proves that during their deposition a pause ensued, and their site became land. Traces of ancient shores, or at least of shallow water, are often preserved in ripple-marked surfaces of sandstones (Fig. 15) on which the trails or burrows of annelides may now and then be observed. If rain-prints (Fig. 16) are associated with rippled surfaces, they conclusively prove the sediment to have accumulated on a shore. Further evidence of the occasional exposure

of the deposits to air and sun is yielded by the desic-
cation-cracks so commonly found among sand-stones
(Fig. 17); while now and then, footprints of birds and
different quadrupeds, impressed on the soft sand, complete the picture of quiet shore-conditions of deposit.
(2) Lacustrine shells and cyprid cases point to former
lakes.   A layer of white marl full of decaying forms of
lymnea, *planorbis*, &c. may often be found below the
grassy surface of a flat meadow.   Such a layer as certainly
demonstrates that the meadow was once a lake, as if we

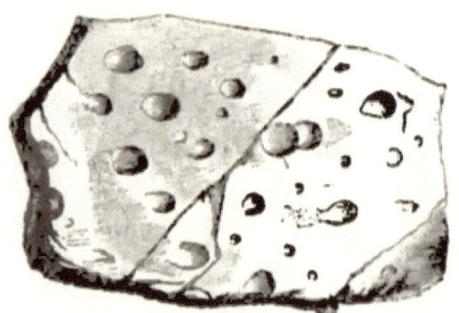

FIG. 16.—Rain-prints on sandstone.

had documentary evidence to prove that such had been
the condition of the place within the last few generations.
(3) Corals, and other zoophytes, mollusca of such genera
as *lingula*, *cyprina*, *buccinum*, and *rissoa*, fishes of, for
example, the ray and shark tribes, point to marine conditions of life.   The conclusion that any particular stratum
must have been laid down on the sea-floor might not be
warranted were it made to rest on merely a single fossil ;
but when the whole character or *facies* of the fossils of a rock
is of a marine type, we may confidently infer that the rock

was deposited on the bed of the sea.   Certain forms of
life have had a remarkable persistence in the ocean.
Some of the living brachiopods, for example, are closely

FIG. 17.—Sun-cracked surface of red sandstone marked with footprints,
Hildburghausen, Saxony.

similar to those even of very early geological periods.
These persistent forms, though they do not absolutely
prove, yet give strong grounds for believing that, as they

are all marine forms now, so they must have been marine from the beginning. And when they are found associated with other forms belonging to recognisable marine types, the inference cannot be resisted.

3. *Terrestrial Movements.*—The importance of organic remains as witnesses of movements of the earth's crust depends upon the limitation of the organisms when living to their own conditions of existence. A group of living sea-shells cannot be found in an inland lake, nor will a living terrestrial vegetation be dredged up from the sea-floor. If, therefore, marine forms of life must be

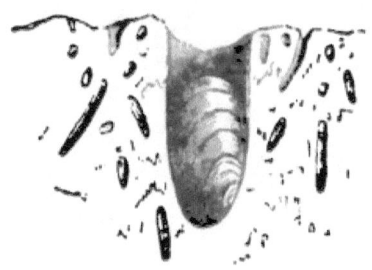

FIG. 18.—Limestone bored by lithodomous shells.

taken as evidence of the presence of the sea and terrestrial forms as proofs of land, we are furnished thereby with an easily applicable and reliable test of change of level between sea and land, and a measure of its minimum amount. A natural terrace of sand and gravel, full of littoral shells, and extending along a coast-line at a height of 100 feet above the present sea-level, shows that sea and land must have shifted relatively to each other to the extent of at least 100 feet. It is generally agreed that in such changes of level it is the land, and not the level of the sea, which

moves up or down.   We say, therefore, that the terrace marks an upheaval of the coast to the extent of
100 feet.   Barnacles adhering to rocks, and living shells
(Fig. 18) which have perforated them, furnish equally satisfactory proofs of a rise of the land.   On the other hand,
a submergence may be demonstrated to have taken place
when a terrestrial surface, with its tree-stumps *in situ*,
old soil and sylvan leaf-mould, is found below high-
water mark.   The trees must have grown above the

FIG. 19.—Section of a buried land-surface (De la Beche). *ee*. rocks underneath;
dd, old vegetable soil; *aa*, stumps of trees still erect in position of growth;
b, prostrate tree-trunk; *cc*, horns of oxen and deer. The whole buried under
silt and modern soil, *f*.

limit of ordinary tidal action, so that the amount of
depression must always more or less exceed the vertical distance between the line of the submerged trees
and the upper edge of the beach.

Among the geological formations which form the visible part of the earth's crust, it is sometimes possible to
obtain instructive sections wherein successive terrestrial
movements and conditions of physical geography are
well illustrated. A good example occurs in Joppa Quarry,

near Edinburgh. It will be seen from the accompanying
section (Fig. 20) that five seams of coal occur, each representing a terrestrial surface, or at least an aquatic floor
whereon grew a vegetation with its roots in the water
and its branches in the air. There must have been
a progressive subsidence until the first formed coal-
seam had been buried under many feet of sand and mud

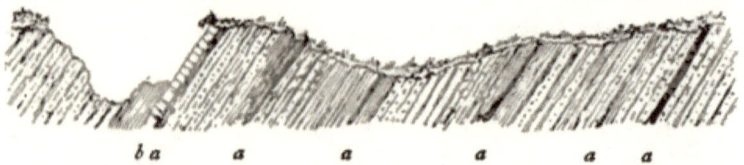

b a   a   a   a   a   a

Fig. 20.—Section of inclined Carboniferous rocks, Joppa Quarry, near Edinburgh.
    a, coal seams; *b*, limestone with marine organisms. The dotted bands are
    sandstones, the shaded are shales and clays.

which inclosed also the remains of other similar terrestrial surfaces. At last, by a more prolonged submergence and the clearing of the water, marine forms of life,
zoophytes, encrinites, and molluscs, made their way into
the area, and flourished so long as to form a bed of limestone about three feet thick. Subsequently the sediment
returned, and as the water was filled up, new coal-growths
sprang up as before.

The observer will find it sometimes possible, by means
of fossil evidence, to prove that strata, apparently in their
natural order, have really been turned upside down, so
that what seems the top of each stratum is really the
bottom. This could be shown if we found in one of
these strata, a row of fossils in their positions of growth,
but with their lower ends uppermost. Suppose, for example, that one stratum contained many erect stems of
trees, and that in every case the roots of these stems

branched out freely at the upper end into an overlying stratum, evidently an old soil.   We could not, in such a case, come to any other conclusion than that the whole of the rocks had been overturned.   Again, instead of a series of land-plants, imagine a number of bunches of coral, with their roots still in the position of growth, but turned up to the sky.   We could only explain that position by admitting that the rocks must have been inverted.

4. *Geological Horizons.*—Fossils have often a high importance in affording to the geologist a clue in his endeavour to unravel the geological structure of a region.   He may discover, for example, that some particular stratum, marked by the occurrence in it of certain fossils, can be recognised and traced over a considerable breadth of ground.   He follows this stratum, using it as a datum-line from which to work out the arrangement of the series both above and below it.   This use of fossils will be more evident when we come to deal in a later chapter with the tracing of geological boundaries, and the working out of geological structure.

5. *Geological Chronology.*—To fix the relative geological position of rocks, and thus to establish a succession or chronology, is doubtless the most important service which fossils render to geology.   Mere resemblances or differences in mineral character are seldom good for great distances.   We cannot always be sure, simply on the ground of general petrographical resemblance, that a group of strata on one side of a country is identical with a similar set on the opposite side.   If they closely resembled each other in that respect, but contained totally distinct fossils, we should

generally conclude, in spite of their outward similarity, that they could not be identified with each other, but must belong to different periods of geological time.   Each great stratified formation of the earth's crust is distinguished by its own characteristic fossils. A method is thus obtainable of recognising the relative geological date of fossiliferous rocks.   To determine and name fossils is the task of the palæontologist. As a rule the field-geologist can do this only to a limited extent, though the greater his power in this respect the more valuable his services in the field.   Part of his train-ing, however, should consist in the study of as good a series of typical fossils as he can consult.   He ought to familiarise his eye with the leading genera and more characteristic species of each geological system and for-mation.   Knowledge of this kind, so portable when carried in the head ready for use, so bulky and difficult to transport and use when contained in many learned volumes, enables him to decide for himself as to the geological horizon of the formations.   Should he be in doubt about the determination of his fossils, he must submit them to an expert in the subject.

For many purposes of field-geology it is not absolutely necessary, though it may be very desirable, that we should know the names and the zoological or botanical grade of the fossils.   What we need to know in the field is that cer-tain organic remains, whatever be their nature or names, occur in particular beds of rock.   We should be able to recognise them and use them as indices to mark out the strata, and thus to fix our geological horizon.   William Smith, by whom this stratigraphical use of fossils was origi-nally taught, knew little of the nomenclature or natural history of the fossils he dealt with. But he learnt to recognise them, and to judge accurately of their position in the geological series, and he made as admirable use of them in tracing the outlines of the development of the Secondary rocks across England as if he had been able to name and describe each species. Geology has made vast strides since his time. Though the field-geologist may use the fossils without any scientific knowledge of them, the sooner he obtains that knowledge the better for his work.   The broad outlines of William Smith's days have to be filled in by more minute and exhaustive work now.

In fine, the field-geologist will find in all quarters of the world that an acquaintance with fossils can be turned to profitable account. It enables him at the outset to fix more or less definitely the relative age of the rocks among which he is engaged and thus affords means of comparison with the corresponding rocks of other countries. Where his labours are of no ambitious kind, but where he works for the quiet pleasure and open-air life of the pursuit, the study of organic remains affords him an endless fund for delightful meditation.   They show him at one place evidence of an old sea-bottom, in the strata where marine remains are crowded together. At another locality they bring before him, in fresh-water shells and other forms, the traces of long-vanished lakes and rivers. At a third spot they reveal, by successive layers of compressed vegetation and hardened loam, the gradual depression and submergence of old forest-covered lands. In such cases they suggest the lines along which his further search should be prosecuted for additional corroborative testimony as to the ancient aspects of the district in which he is at work.   The land-plants, for example, lead him to look for fresh-water forms of life, for sun-cracked and rain-pitted surfaces of rock ; while the occurrence of marine forms of life prompts to search for other proofs of the ancient encroachments of the sea.

CHAPTER VIII.

WHETHER or not the observer sets about the construction of a map, he can form but a limited notion of the geology of a country if he confines his attention merely to a few quarries or lines of natural section. Having learned in such openings what is the nature and order of succession of the rocks, he ought to try to follow them out, from where they are clearly seen into other parts of the country, and in so doing, endeavour to note as he goes any variation in character which they may present, and every feature which serves to indicate what must be the disposition of the rocks below.

A very short experience of geological work in the field suffices to show the observer that over wide spaces he cannot actually see what rock lies beneath him. He may get an admirable section laid bare in some ravine or brook, or by the shore of the sea : but beyond the limits of this section the ground may be deeply buried under vegetation, soil, sand, gravel, clay, or other superficial formation, and no other section may occur for an interval of, it may be, several miles. Yet he must form some conclusion as to the nature of the rocks between these places.

In cases of this kind information may often be obtained from an examination of the soil. What we call vegetable soil is merely the upper stratum of decayed rock mixed with vegetable and animal remains. (Fig. 21.) It commonly betrays its origin by the still undecomposed fragments of stone mixed through its mass. In one tract, for instance, we may find it full of pieces of sandstone, to

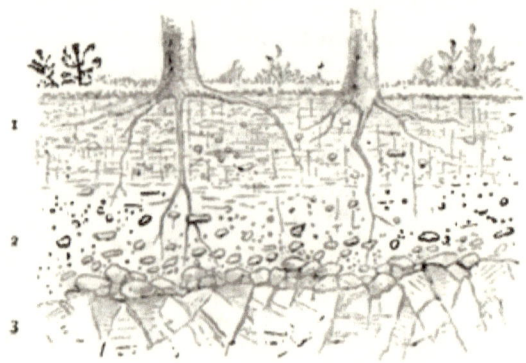

FIG 21.—Section to show the superficial covering of soil (1), subsoil (2) derived from the disintegration of the underlying rock (3).

the exclusion perhaps of every other kind of rock. If the land has been under cultivation, the sandstone may be in large pieces, where it has been turned up by the plough. We should there infer with some confidence that sandstone lay underneath *in situ.* If again the soil were a stiff red loam or clay, with few or no stones, it would indicate the existence of some red marl or clay immediately underneath. A sandy soil full of well-rounded, water-worn stones, would show the presence of some gravelly deposit below. A calcareous soil full of blocks of flint would probably indicate the existence of chalk. A stiff argillaceous soil, abounding in smoothed stones, many of them well-striated, would prove that a boulder-clay or till lay below. A profusion of fragments of some peculiar rock, a basalt, for example, or a diorite, or a porphyrite, extending in a definite band across a field or hill-side, would probably show us that a rock of that character existed, *in situ*, somewhere in the immediate neighbourhood of the fragments. We require, of course, in all these cases, to go carefully over the ground, and draw our conclusion only after we have exhausted all the evidence procurable.

But it may be remarked that, except on freshly-ploughed land, the soil is not bare and exposed to our scrutiny; that, on the contrary, it is commonly just as much concealed by its coating of vegetation as the hard rocks are by their covering of soil. Even under the most unfavourable circumstances, however, the geologist may often be able to learn not a little of the information he needs. Where the ground has a slope he will probably have no great trouble in finding some little rut or trench which has been cut, or at least deepened, by rain, and where he will obtain access to the underlying soil, or even, it may be, to the subsoil and the still undecomposed rock below it. Where, on the other hand, the ground is too flat to hope for assistance from rain-action, he will look for traces of burrowing animals, by which the soil may have been thrown up to the surface. In Britain the common earth-worm, the mole, and the rabbit, are excellent coadjutors in his work. The fine castings of the earth-worm give him at least the colour and general constitution of the soil, whether sandy or clayey. The heaps of the

mole include the smaller stones in the soil, and permit
an inference to be drawn as to the probable nature of
the materials from the decomposition of which the soil
has been formed.   The extensive excavations of the
rabbit lay bare not only the constitution of the soil, but
often also the angular *débris* which rests immediately
upon the solid rock.

From vegetation, also, the field-geologist learns to
draw many a shrewd inference as to the character of the
soil and rock below.   A spring, or line of springs, indicative of some geological boundary line such as the

Fig. 22.—Section of a valley showing the outcrop of a junction of sandstone
and shale marked by a line of springs, *s, s.*

junction of a harder or softer stratum (Fig. 22), or a
line of fracture (Fig. 34), will reveal itself by marshy
ground or by a brighter green along a hill slope.   The
course of a limestone band or a basalt dyke may be
followed, by the peculiar verdure of its vegetable covering,
across a moorland where little or no solid rock may be
seen.   A ridge of serpentine stands up bare and rough,
affording at best but an unkindly soil for plant-growth.
Trees, too, change with the varying character of the
rocks on which they grow.   Each country presents its
own illustrations of these relations, which must be
gradually learnt and made to give their assistance to the
observer's progress.

In judging of the probable character of the rocks

underneath from the nature of the overlying soil, the
geologist will, of course, be guided by the local circumstances in every case. For example, if the surface of
the ground should present many rounded pebbles and
boulders, he will not at once conclude that these fragments have been derived from the rock *in situ* below.
Their rounded forms will rather raise a suspicion that
they have been transported, and should many of them
plainly show the characteristic smoothed surface of water-
worn stones, they will be set down as derived immediately
from some adjacent bed of gravel or conglomerate. The
mere fact of a great variety of rounded rock-fragments
occurring over the surface at any locality, suggests a mass
of transported material, rather than the decomposition
of the solid rocks underneath.

On the other hand, the occurrence of abundant angular
fragments of rock on the surface, at once arrests attention,
as indicative of the vicinity of that rock *in situ*. The
observer traverses the ground in all directions in search
of any projecting knob of the actual rock itself. Failing
to find it, he notes the position of these angular chips,
and tries whether they can be traced further, so as to
indicate by their distribution at the surface the probable
trend of the solid rock underneath. In ascending a hill-
side so covered with trains of detritus or vegetation that
no rock can be seen in place, the geologist may learn
much regarding the concealed rocks by examining the
débris. He knows that the fragments of stone have all
rolled down, and not up. When, therefore, in his ascent,
he observes that the angular chips of some particular
rock, abundant enough below, no longer appear, he surmises that he must have crossed the limits of the solid

rock which furnished the fragments. If in the course of subsequent examination he discovers that those fragments disappear about the same line all along the hill, he may regard his first surmise as probably correct, and draw a boundary line accordingly, even although he may never have seen the actual rock itself *in situ*.

Again, in the ascent of streams similar close observation and sagacious inference will often go far to supply the place of actual sections of rock. The use of the evidence in these cases, however, requires still more caution than on the bare hill-side, because the tendency of running water is to round the rock fragments exposed to it, and hence in the channel of a brook or river, it may not be always possible to distinguish between the pebbles which came as angular fragments from neighbouring solid rocks, and have been rounded by the attrition of the brook or river itself, and those which, derived from some old gravel, were already rounded and water-worn before they tumbled into the channel. A great abundance of fragments of one particular variety of rock, however, would suggest that they had not been washed out of some gravel bed, but had been derived from the waste of a solid rock lying somewhat further up in the drainage basin of the stream. In such a case, moreover, the proportion of these fragments in the channel would probably be found to increase as the stream was traced upwards. Perhaps they might be observed, too, to become larger in size and less water-worn the further they were followed up the stream. If they should suddenly cease, the observer should at once note the fact, as possibly indicating that the rock did not occur higher up, but had its upper limit somewhere near the point where the fragments in the stream disappeared. While these particular rock-chips ceased, others of some different rock might be found to increase in number, and another zone of rock might be shown and traced in a similar way.

In nothing is the highest type of a field-geologist better displayed than in the exhaustiveness and sagacity with which, in the absence of all other evidence, these various little indications of the geology of a district are sought for, found, and marshalled in their proper places, so as to bear witness to the distribution and probable structure of the rocks. Such an observer would be able in many cases to trace lines, with a near approach to accuracy, over ground which a less skilled student would pronounce to be a blank.

It must often happen, however, that the ground is so obscured by superficial accumulations, such as vegetation, soil, gravel, and clay, that no indication whatever can for considerable intervals be found as to the nature of the solid rocks underneath. Under these circumstances the geologist, when no boring or mining operations are at his service, must do the best he can, by examining all the surrounding ground, to determine what lies below the concealed area. And in the great majority of cases he can form a tolerably correct surmise as to the general nature and disposition of the rocks. To do this requires some knowledge of geological structure, which we shall consider in the following chapter.

CHAPTER IX.

THE UNRAVELLING OF GEOLOGICAL STRUCTURE.—DIP, STRIKE, OUTCROP.

IF we could only recognise the rocks, where actually seen, but form no satisfactory conclusion regarding their distribution under a concealing mantle of vegetation or superficial detritus ; if we could tell the arrangement and measure the thickness of strata only at the surface, but offer no opinion as to the prolongation of these strata underground, we should never know much about the crust of the earth, and certainly could do comparatively little to advance geological inquiry. Fortunately it is not only possible but comparatively easy to pronounce upon the subterranean arrangement of rocks from indications obtainable at the surface. We seldom need to bore or dig. It is usually enough if we can avail ourselves of the surface evidence, and gain from it information respecting the probable arrangement of the rocks below, or in other words, the geological structure of the ground. How this is done, let us now proceed to consider.

Horizontal.Strata.—Outcrop.—In a region where the rocks are all horizontal, only the uppermost stratum may be seen, in which case an example of extreme simplicity of structure would result. There would then be no outcrop or exposed edge of any stratum to be traced, unless the surface of the ground should be so uneven as to expose the edges of lower strata. Except in tracts of low alluvium, however, horizontal strata have usually been more or less trenched by valleys and ravines, so that sections are laid bare of the underlying beds, while the surface of the country seldom rigidly corresponds with the surface of a stratum, but has been worn across it, so as here and there to leave " outliers " or outstanding portions of this upper stratum, and to lay bare the strata below. Where this has taken place in bare hilly land, with abundance of exposures of the rocks, although the geological structure is still of the simplest possible kind, considerable practice and skill may be needed to follow the exposed edges or outcrops of the strata, and to delineate them accurately, and at the same time artistically, upon a map. The accompanying drawings (Fig. 23) may serve to illustrate how very tortuous the outcrops of perfectly horizontal beds may be, should the ground be much varied in outline, and especially by the occurrence of wide and deep valleys. In the uppermost map (A) a representation is given of horizontal rocks deeply trenched by valleys and ravines. In the lower map (B) the inequalities of the ground are much less, yet even in such a gently undulating district the outcrops of horizontal strata may evidently run in remarkably sinuous lines.

I have used the word artistic with reference to the tracing of geological boundary-lines, and have done so advisedly. Where the rocks are all visible, the observer

has only to follow nature, and the more faithfully he does
so, the more graceful will his lines probably be.   The
curves produced by denudation, though often complex,

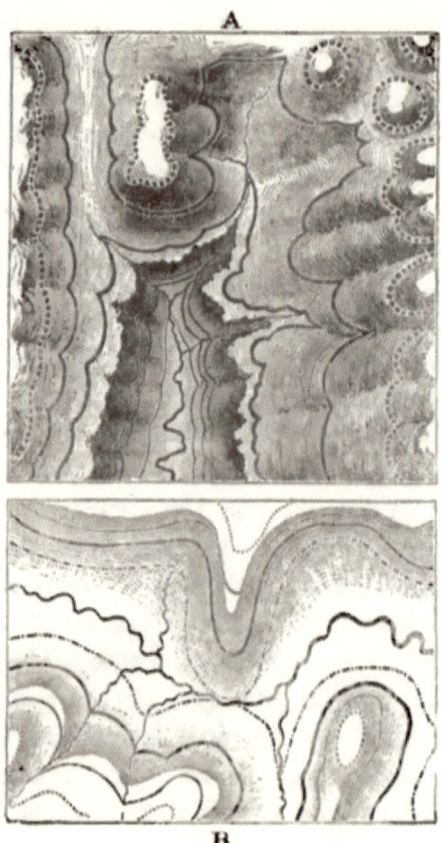

FIG. 23.—Sinuous outcrops of horizontal strata depending on inequalities of
surface.

are never awkward and inharmonious.   Where the rocks
are not seen, and where therefore the position of the
boundary-lines must be inferred, the surveyor will follow

the analogies of his district and run his boundaries with the same kind of flowing lines which he sees them to possess where they can be actually examined.   Two men may map the same piece of ground quite correctly as regards its general structure, but the map of the one will show by the complexity of its lines and the fidelity with which they follow the varieties of the surface configuration, how faithfully and skilfully the work has been done ; while the map of the other will indicate that its author, though marking correctly the general structure, has failed to recognise, or, at least, to express the relations of that structure to external form.   The former map will in most cases be a far more artistic as well as accurate production than the latter.   Not only in such simple work as the tracing of horizontal strata, but in all the details of geological map-making, the artistic eye and hand have scope to show their presence : to the great advantage of the maps to which they are applied.

Inclined Strata.—Dip.—Instead of lying quite flat, however, stratified rocks are usually inclined to the horizon.   This inclination, called their *dip*, is measured as to its direction by the compass, as to its angle by the

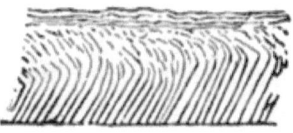

Fig. 24.—True dip concealed by superficial disturbance of the strata.

clinometer.   In determining these points it is always desirable to see more than a mere projecting edge of rock, for sometimes what seems to be the dip in such a case is deceptive.   In Fig. 24, for instance, the rocks are

really inclined at a high angle towards the left hand. Yet
if seen merely at the surface where they have been bent
back (by the slide of rubbish down-hill, or by a grinding
mass of ice or other superficial agent) they might be
supposed to be dipping from left to right. To be sure
of the true angle and direction, we must not be content

FIG. 25.—Inclined strata appearing horizontal when exposed at a right angle
to the dip.

with one small face of rock, but should go round a section until we determine the point satisfactorily. A face
of rock, for instance, seen from one side, as in Fig. 25,
may appear to be made of horizontal strata, which from
another point of view are found to be considerably inclined. The direction of dip will always be at a right
angle to the line along which the edges of the inclined
beds appear horizontal. Failing, therefore, to find any

actual section along the true line of dip, we should so place ourselves as to have the exposed edges of the strata running in horizontal bars in front of us. We may then take the direction of dip with the compass, and determine from the mean of a number of observations taken with the clinometer on projecting ledges what must be the general average angle of dip. The best measurements of the angle of dip are made when we can place ourselves some little distance in front of a face of rock which has been cut in the true direction of dip. We can then place the clinometer in front of our eye, and make its edge coincide with the line of a particular stratum many yards in extent. Thus in one single observation we obviate the risks of error where only small ledges of the inclined beds can be used. Where the true dip cannot be directly measured we may, by measuring the apparent dip of two faces of rock inclined at a considerable angle to each other, obtain the true dip by calculation.[1]

Having ascertained these particulars, we insert the information in our note-book or map. The use of a map for the registering of observations on geological structure requires an amount of precision which might not be thought needful for the pages of a note-book, and secures in consequence the most careful and exhaustive kind of field-work. I shall, therefore, suppose in what I have to say on this part of my subject, that we are required not

---

[1] Rules are given for measuring or calculating the dip. (See Green's *Geology*, p. 341.) For almost all practical purposes, however, a good field-geologist can get his angle with the clinometer in the field by selecting, as he learns how to do, his points of observation.

only to make observations on geological structure, but to
formulate them on paper, and to construct the geological
map of a region.

The usual sign used on geological maps to express the
dip of strata is an arrow pointing in the direction of inclination (the direction being found on paper by help of
an ordinary protractor), with the number of degrees of
angle shown in figures at the side of it. We place,
therefore, an arrow at each point on the map where
we ascertain the dip of strata. A glance at the map
(Figs. 26 & 27) will show how this is done. Each arrow
marks the site of the observation, and with its accompanying figures records the result. Where possible we
enter beside the arrow some symbols, or contracted
writing, to describe the nature of the rock, or any other
particulars which it seems desirable to record. Further
detail, where required, finds its place in the note-book.

Selection of Horizons—Mapping of Outcrop.—As it is
impossible on any ordinary map to represent every bed
of rock, the geologist must decide what beds should be
selected to be traced out. This cannot always be done
until considerable progress has been made with the work.
The selection must depend not merely upon the geological or industrial importance of the beds, but also, and
not less frequently, upon the extent to which they are
exposed and capable of being followed across the district.
A particular stratum of no special interest in itself may
come to have a high importance as a geological horizon
or platform if it is easily recognisable, and from its thickness, hardness, or other peculiarity, stands out so prominently that it can be satisfactorily traced from point to point
for a long distance. Such stratigraphically serviceable

bands may be found in most districts of stratified rocks
Great assistance in the tracing of horizons is likewise
afforded by organic remains, as has been already pointed
out. A particular stratum, even when thin and otherwise of no apparent importance, may acquire a high
value if it is charged with fossils, and can be recognised
over a wide area.

The outcrop may be marked at any particular locality
by a short line beside the dip-arrow, or if the outcrop be
a broad one, by two lines, one marking the base, the
other the top of the band. The space between two such
lines—in other words, the breadth of the outcrop—is
determined by the thickness of the bed or beds, their
angle of inclination, and the slope or contour of the
ground. Among a series of vertical strata the breadth
of the outcrop of a bed corresponds exactly with the
true thickness of that bed. The more the angle of
inclination lessens, the broader does the outcrop at the
surface become. Hence, in tracing such a band across
a country, attention must constantly be given to the
variations of angle in the dip. Where the dip increases
the band narrows in breadth; where the dip lessens the
band widens. This is best seen on level or gently undulating ground; it is apt to be less distinctly shown where
the ground is very uneven, and where therefore constant
modifications of the line of outcrop are produced, as we
have seen to be the case with horizontal strata. When
strata are vertical no amount of surface irregularity
makes any difference on their outcrop. They are apt
in that position to run on for some distance with little
deviation of direction, so that the outcrop of one of them
might be marked by a straight bar or line (Fig. 26). The

Fig. 26.—Map showing the data from which a completed geological map is made. (The top of the map is north.)

influence of the form of the ground tells more and more upon the outcrop in proportion as the strata approach the horizontal.

Strike.—The outcrop of a stratum is the line which that stratum makes with the surface of the ground. This term "outcrop" is often spoken of as if it were the same as the "strike." The latter word is applied to a line drawn perpendicular to the direction of dip. It is the line made by a stratum with the horizon, and shows the general or average direction of that stratum across the country. On a perfectly level piece of ground strike and outcrop must obviously coincide, and there must likewise be a complete coincidence among vertical strata. The more irregular the surface, and the less inclined the strata, the further must strike and outcrop depart from each other.

Relation of Strike to Dip.—There is a further relation to be noted as we proceed, viz.—the constant dependence of the direction of strike upon that of dip, and the consequent changes of strike as the direction of dip varies. The strike is of course a mathematical line cutting the dip at a right angle. If the dip is east or west, the strike must be north and south; if the dip is north or south, the strike must be east and west. It must not be supposed, however, that the line of strike is always, or even most commonly, a straight one. It can only be so as long as the direction of dip continues unchanged. But a comparatively brief experience in the field suffices to show how constantly the dip of strata varies, now to one side, now to another, every such variation producing a corresponding change upon the line of strike. Where the deviations are slight, and of local character, while the mean direction of inclination remains ·the same, we take that mean direction as governing the strike (as at band F in Fig. 27). Where, on the other hand, the dip is to different points of the compass in succession over wide spaces, we connect the arrows on our map by lines (as in band G in Fig. 27), and find that the strike becomes a curved, and even, it may be, a very sinuous one.

Difference between Outcrop and Strike.—These two terms ought to be distinguished, otherwise, in constructing a geological map, we shall either lose the impression of the external form of the ground, which a correctly-traced outcrop so often vividly conveys, or we shall be in danger of regarding the dip as constantly changing, and the strata, though perhaps nearly flat, as extensively disturbed. Looking at any good geological map of England and Wales, that by Sir Andrew C. Ramsay, for example, the reader will notice that the bands of the Oolitic and Cretaceous rocks, while retaining a tolerably persistent strike from south-west to north east, across the breadth of the country, present a most sinuous and irregular edge. The direction of the dip, and consequently the trend of the strike, change but little, yet it will be observed that the outcrop is continually shifting to-and-fro. The strata really follow each other in parallel bands. If we could plane down the whole country to a dead level, these bands would be marked by alternate strips of clays, limestones, and sandy rocks. But instead of being a flat, the country undulates, and hence a series of gently inclined rocks of very various degrees of durability necessarily gives a diversified set of outcrops. No better illustration could

be studied of the difference between outcrop and strike,
and of the marked influence even of small ridges and
hollows and shallow valleys upon the outcrop of strata,
where the angle of dip is low. The main facts to be
expressed upon the map of such a tract of country are,
that the formations follow each other in a certain order,
and cross the region in a certain direction. Of course we
might record these facts by simply drawing straight
parallel strips across the map, each marking the position
and relative breadth of one of the formations.   This
was the way in which the old geological maps on a
small scale were constructed.   The map of England and
Wales in Bakewell's *Geology*, even so late as the edition
of 1838, may serve as an example.   But by such a style
of mapping we entirely lose, as I have just said, one of
the valuable features of a geological map—the relation
between the form of the ground and the nature and outline of the rocks below, that is, between scenery and
geological structure.   It may readily be believed that
this is too important a relation to be ignored without
great disadvantage when the scale of the map at all
permits it to be expressed.   Besides, the omission
deprives the map of the chief feature by which the
skilled and artistic observer is distinguished from him
whose eye and hand are less quick to seize upon and
delineate the characteristic varieties of form which geological boundaries assume as the surface of a country
changes from plain to hill, and as the rocks themselves
alter in thickness and position.

Numerous illustrations of the applicability of this prin-
ciple will occur to every observer in the field.   If, for example, he stands at the higher margin of a rocky valley,

along the sides of which inclined beds of sandstone,
limestone, or other stratified rocks are exposed, dipping
gently down the valley, he observes that when the outcrop of each bed reaches the edge of the declivity it
does not go straight on to the corresponding outcrop on
the opposite side.   On the contrary, it descends the
slope in a slant until it reaches the bottom of the valley,
when it turns and mounts the opposite slope, thus forming a V-shaped indentation on the general line of strike
(as in the valleys on the south side of the map, Figs. 26
and 27).   Now the manner in which these windings of the
outcrop of inclined strata and their relation to the form
of the ground are expressed upon the geological map is
a good test of the skill and delicacy which I have insisted
upon as so desirable in the map-work of a field-geologist.
Many observers are content to draw the lines of outcrop as straight bars across the valleys, thus making
them coincident with the strike.   On maps of a small
scale, indeed, nothing else is possible.   But where the
scale admits of it, much advantage may be gained by
faithfully depicting the curving outcrops.   The map then
tells its story at once, and brings the relation between
geological structure and external form as vividly before
the eye as a well-made model could do.

   Construction of a Geological Map.—In order to show
the application of the foregoing remarks, two diagrams
(Figs. 26 and 27) are given.   In Fig. 26 an attempt
is made to convey some idea of the way in which
the data are compiled and recorded in the construction of a geological map.   The shaded parts of that
figure represent what is actually seen by the geologist:
over the blank portions he is supposed to have been

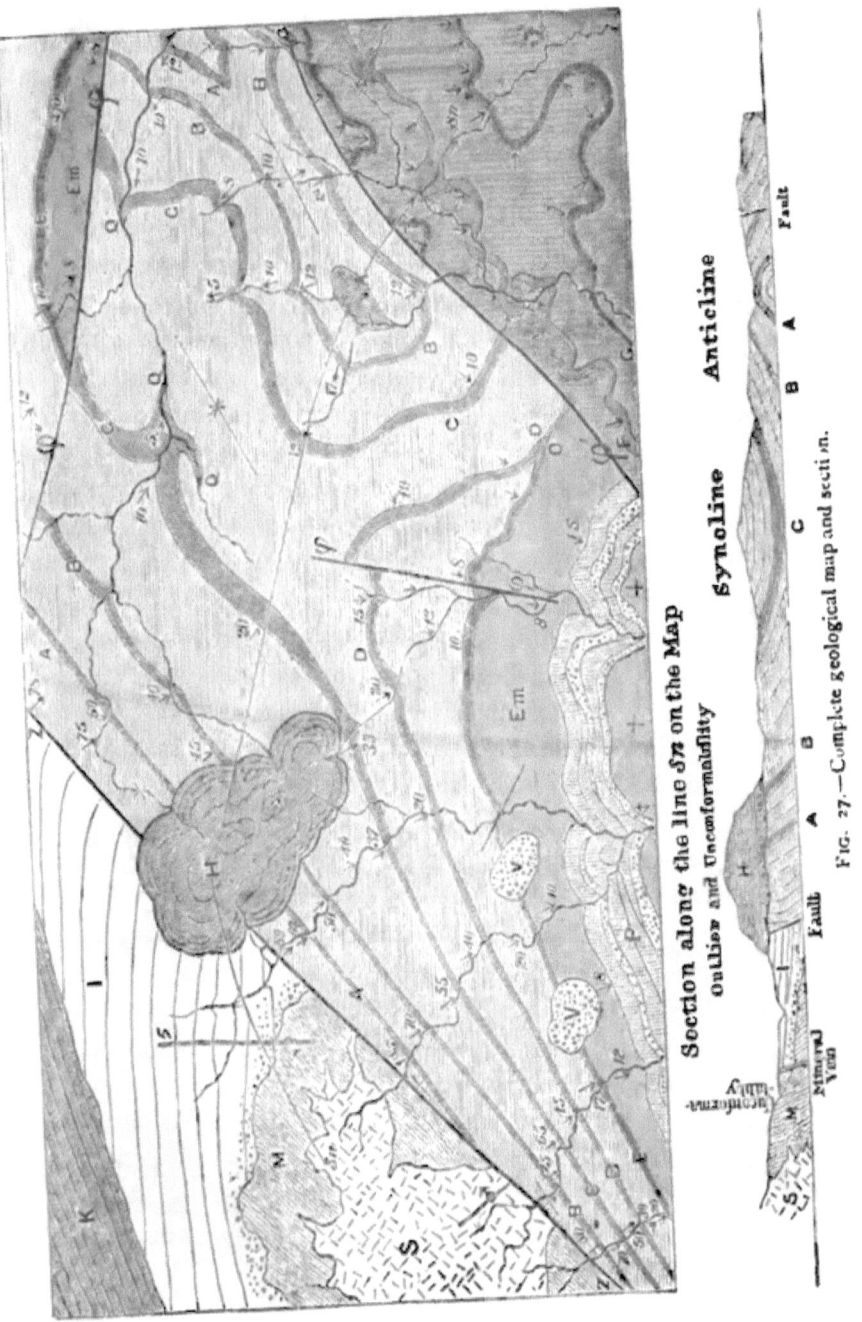

Section along the line *Sn* on the Map

Outliers and Unconformability

Synoline   Anticline

Fault   Mineral
Vein

Unconformability

Fault

FIG. 27.—Complete geological map and section.

unable to find any rock *in situ*. Fig. 27 shows the map as filled in and completed from these data. I shall have occasion to make frequent references to these maps in what follows.

It will be noticed that most of the observations occur along the stream-courses, these being the most frequent natural lines of section. At each point where the dip of strata has been taken, an arrow and number mark the direction and angle. The more important or strati-graphically serviceable beds have their outcrop marked in decided lines where it is actually seen. When the same stratum can be recognised in two parallel or adjacent streams or valleys, the outcrop may be drawn across the intervening ground, which of course should itself be searched for traces of the desired line. Where there can be no doubt as to the direction and position of the out-crop, it may be drawn as a continuous line or band. Where, however, though it is known to occur within certain limits, some doubt may exist as to its exact position, it should be expressed by broken or dotted lines.

Establishing a Stratigraphical order of Succession.—It will be seen from the map that in the streams at the lower part of the left side, the same beds are recognisable, following and dipping under each other at corresponding intervals. In other words, the order of succession is found to be the same in the different streams. Bed *A* after an interval is followed by bed *B*, bed *B* by bed *C*, and so on. Even, therefore, where a blank space occurs, and, owing to some surface accumulation, a particular bed may not be visible in one of the lines of section, we can be tolerably sure of the place where, judging from the strata above and below, it would be seen if it came to the surface. We do not hesitate, therefore, to draw dotted lines across that place to indicate our belief A geological map is thus derived partly from what is seen, and partly from what can be legitimately inferred.

I would further direct attention to the fact that while the order in which the beds occur remains the same in all the streams upon our map (Figs. 26 and 27), the spaces between them vary considerably. This difference may arise from one or other of three causes; either (1) variation in angle of dip, or (2) variation in thickness of strata, or (3) inequalities in the level of the ground. We have already considered the effect of a decrease of inclination in increasing the breadth of a stratum or series of strata at the surface of the ground. It is further evident that if the mass of strata between two known beds should swell out or diminish, the breadth of the space between their respective outcrops must correspondingly vary. Inequalities of the surface must likewise influence, as we have seen, not only the direction of the outcrops, but also their breadth. Where, therefore, the angle of dip does not change, and the surface of the ground presents no marked inequalities, but where, nevertheless, a decided widening or narrowing of the interval between two outcrops occurs, we infer with confidence that the intermediate strata must increase or diminish in thickness.

Estimation of Thickness of Strata.—When the angles of dip have been observed along a line perpendicular to the strike, it is easy to calculate what the thickness of rock must be in any given interval of the section, or to obtain it by using the protractor. This is most conveniently done at home, where the observer can collect his notes and protract the angles he has taken in the field.

It is useful, however, to have a ready means of estimating thickness, and in this respect the following rule, given by Mr. Charles Maclaren,[1] will be found of service. If the breadth of inclined strata is measured across their outcrop at right angles to the strike, their true thickness will be equal to $\frac{1}{12}$th of their breadth at the surface for every 5° of dip. Or it may be put thus: divide 60 by the angle of dip, and the fraction is obtained which expresses the thickness. Thus, suppose a mass of strata measures across the strike 1,200 feet, and is uniformly inclined at an angle of 5°, its real thickness will be $\frac{1}{12}$th, or 100 feet; at 10° the thickness will be $\frac{1}{6}$th, or 200 feet; at 15° it will be $\frac{1}{4}$th, or 300 feet; at 20°, $\frac{1}{3}$rd, or 400 feet. This rule is very nearly accurate for inclinations up to 45°.

Thinning away of Strata.—Overlap.—It sometimes happens that two lines of outcrop come together, owing to the complete thinning away of the intermediate strata, and the conjoined outcrops may then be traceable for a long distance without further change. Instances of this

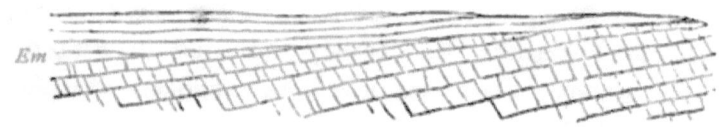

D

FIG. 28.—Section of an overlap.

kind sometimes occur among the coal-seams of coalfields. The higher portions of a series of strata now and then steal over the lower, so as to constitute what is termed an "overlap." This structure cannot always be

[1] Maclaren's *Geology of Fife and the Lothians*, p. xv.

expressed in plan upon a map, but is made clear by a
section. On the map (Fig. 27) the upper portions of the
group *Em* overlaps upon group *D* in the neighbourhood
of the locality marked *O*. A section of this part of the
district would be as in Fig. 28.

This structure may frequently be met with along the
margins of formations deposited in tracts which were
undergoing gradual submergence. As the land sank,
successive zones were carried down beneath the sea,
and the later deposits of the sea-floor were prolonged
further and further beyond the limits of the earlier ones.

Fig. 29.—Overlap and unconformability, Mendip Hills (De la Beche). *c*, Old
Red Sandstone : *b*, Lower Limestone Shale :*a*,*a*.Carboniferous Limestone :
d, beach deposits of Lower Jurassic age passing up into *e* Lias ; *f*, Sands of
Inferior Oolite, which are overlapped by *g*, *n*, Inferior Oolite ; *h*, *l*, clay,
and *i*, limestone of Fuller's earth.

The accompanying section (Fig. 29) shows very clearly
an overlap among the Jurassic beds, all of which lie unconformably on the palæozoic rocks.

Unconformability.—In an overlap the strata are parts
of one continuous unbroken series, the formation of
which does not appear to have been interrupted by any
great physical disturbance, nor even in many cases by
marked change of any kind in the general conditions of
deposit. But where the accumulation of a group of
rocks has been succeeded by its elevation, exposure, and
denudation, the next set of rocks laid down upon it
are said to lie unconformably ; and this kind of junction

is termed an unconformability. Thus in Fig. 29 the
Secondary formations (d—i) lie unconformably upon the
Palæozoic rocks (a—c). It is not necessary that the older
rocks should have been disturbed from their original
horizontality—they may have been equally upraised,
and, after being exposed to denudation, may have been
equally depressed again. It usually happens, however,
that some tilt has been given to them, and consequently
that the overlying rocks rest transgressively upon their
upturned and worn edges.

An unconformable junction is of the highest importance in the geological structure of a district. It marks
one of the great gaps or intervals in geological history.
The observer ought to spare no pains to collect all the
available data in every case where he has reason to
suspect the existence of such a structure.

An extreme case presents little difficulty. It can be
expressed so clearly upon a map as at once to tell its
own story. Thus in Fig. 27 the sheet of rock *H*
evidently forms a flat unconformable cake lying upon
inclined and denuded strata. A section across this
cake would disclose an abrupt junction of the horizontal beds on the edges of the steep and vertical series
But many cases occur where the discordance between
the two series is far less strong, where indeed much
care and labour may be required to make out an unconformability at all. For here again, as in the case
of faults, the actual line of contact between the two
groups of rocks is comparatively seldom seen. We must
usually infer from their general arrangement and their
relations to each other whether or not they are separated
by an unconformability. In the diagram we have already

used so much (Fig. 27) another and less violent unconformability is shown towards the north-west corner, where
the series of beds *K* steals over the denuded outcrops of
the series *I.*

In collecting evidence on the subject of a supposed
unconformability the observer should endeavour to realize
to himself what must have been the contour of the
ground at the time when the overlying rocks were accumulated. He may in this way sometimes be led to
see that his suspected unconformability is extremely un-
likely, or physically impossible. As a curious illustration

Fig. 30.—Portion of a geological section with an impossible unconformability.

of the consequences of the want of this precaution Fig.
30 is here inserted from a recently published geological
section. The horizontal distance represented is about
six miles, and as the upper rocks are made to dip at
angles of between 40° and 50°, there must be a mass of
them somewhere about four and a half miles thick. If
we suppose them to have been originally perfectly horizontal, they must have been laid down against the
slopes of a mountain about four and a half miles high ; or
if they sloped gently away from the underlying rocks, the
height of the mountain must have been still greater.
But not only, however, must a stupendous mountain have
been tilted round so as to lie on its side, but the whole
of the later rocks must have been removed except a

I

narrow cake cut across the bedding parallel with the
original slope of the mountain.   In reality there are
not two sets of rocks in the line of section.   The
whole is one, subject here and there to local crumpling, as might have been seen by more careful and
extended observation.

In most cases it is possible so to express an unconformable junction upon the map as to make it readily
apparent to the geologist.   It should be the aim of the
surveyor to neglect no item of evidence which will enable
him to do this ; for the more perfectly his map is self-in
terpreting, the more useful will it be.   Hence where, as is
often the case, the ground is obscured by surface-accumu-
lations, and a little liberty of choice is left to him as to
the precise course along which to place his line of unconformability, he will draw his line in such a way as to
show as clearly as may be that it is not a fault or an
ordinary conformable junction.

In some districts, particularly in those where older formations are covered by more recent superficial accumulations, a double unconformability may often be seen.
The accompanying diagram, for example (Fig. 31), represents what is exposed in a cliff section at Cullen, on
the coast of Banffshire.   The lowest formation consists
of quartz-rock (*q*) in strata inclined at a high angle to
the south-east.   Their upturned ends are unconformably
overlaid by red sandstones and conglomerates (*s*) dipping
gently away towards the south-west.   These beds are in
turn unconformably covered by the glacial clays and
gravels (*d*).   This is an interesting and instructive
section, inasmuch as it teaches us how rash it would be
to form any conclusion as to the relative length of the

intervals of time represented by the amount of discordance between unconformable formations. The break between the quartz-rock and the red sandstones is apparently much more violent and complete than that between
the sandstones and the glacial deposits. And yet there

Fig. 31.—Double unconformability at Cullen, Banffshire.

can be no doubt that in regard to geological age, the
interval between the deposition of the quartz-rocks and
that of the sandstones was greatly shorter than that
between the sandstones and the overlying clays and
gravels. It is evident indeed that sections might be

found showing an apparently perfect conformability for a certain space between the sandstones and the glacial beds. Yet this local agreement in position would not be allowed to conceal the real and complete break between the two series of formations.

CHAPTER X.

THE UNRAVELLING OF GEOLOGICAL STRUCTURE

FAULTS.

WE have been dealing hitherto only with such variations in the outcrop of strata as may arise from the form
of the ground, from variations in the thickness of beds
or from changes in the direction and angle of dip. But
the outcrop is often broken completely across, and even
removed entirely out of sight, by those dislocations in
the earth's crust to which the name of "faults" has
been given by geologists. These lines of fracture generally form little or no feature at the surface, so that their
existence would commonly not be suspected. They
comparatively rarely appear in visible sections, but are
apt rather to conceal themselves under surface accumulations just at those points in a ravine or other natural
section where we might hope to catch them. Yet they
undoubtedly constitute one of the most important features in the geological structure of a district or country,
and should consequently be traced with the greatest
care.

The learner may, perhaps, hesitate to believe that a
geologist can satisfactorily trace a line of fracture which

he never actually sees.   But a little attention to this part
of our subject will, I hope, convince him that the mere
visible section of a fault on some cliff or shore does not
afford by any means such clear evidence of its nature
and effects as may be obtained from other parts of the
region where it does not show itself at the surface at all.
In fact he might be deceived by a single section with a
fault exposed in it, and might be led to regard that fault
as an important and dominant one, while it might be
only a secondary dislocation in the near neighbourhood
of a great fracture, for which the evidence would be
elsewhere obtainable, but which might never be seen
itself.   The actual position (within a few yards) of a
large fault, its line across the country, its effect on the
surface, its influence on geological structure, its amount
of vertical displacement at different parts of its course—
all this information may be admirably worked out, and
yet the actual fracture may never be seen in any one
single section on the ground.   A visible exposure of the
fracture would be interesting; it would give the exact
position of the line at that particular place; but it would
not be necessary to prove the existence of the fault, nor
would it perhaps furnish any additional information of
importance.

The geologist, therefore, constantly finds evidence of
far more dislocations than he can actually see.   Those
which appear, sometimes commonly enough on lines of
cliff or coast-section, are apt to be but small and trifling
The larger faults—those which powerfully influence the
geological structure of a country—are seldom to be
caught in any such visible form.   Now why is this?
Different reasons may be assigned, each of weight.

First of all, it is evident that along lines of great dislocation there must have been, on the whole, greater
pressure, and greater grinding and fracture of the fis-
sure-walls than in clean, sharp cracks, where the rocks
have been displaced only a few feet or yards. The
broken rock in the line of fault crumbles down more
than the solid rock on either side beyond it, or is more
easily excavated and removed. So that whether on a
cliff or on a flat surface, the actual fault is apt to be concealed by superficial detritus. Then again, large faults
often bring together rocks of considerably different
degrees of durability. The less-lasting material decom-
poses, and its *débris* goes to cover the actual junction-

Fig. 32.—Section of lias (*a*), and new red sandstone and marl (*b*), cut by faults
(*f f*), near Watchet, Bristol Channel. (De la Beche.)

line between the two formations. Another reason may be
sought in the extensive deposits of gravel, clay, or other
superficial materials which are spread over the surface of
a country and conceal the solid rocks. A line of fault
is one of weakness, presenting facilities for attack by the
denuding forces whereby it is hollowed out, so as to
become a receptacle for these superficial deposits. In
the vast majority of cases faults produce no visible change
on the contour of the surface. This shows how extensively the ground has everywhere been planed down by
denuding agencies. In the foregoing section (Fig. 32),
for example, five faults are shown ; yet in no single case
does the line of dislocation betray itself by any marked
surface feature.

In the consideration of faults, therefore, two questions obviously arise. How does a geologist recognise faults when he sees them? and how does he prove their existence when he does not, and cannot, see them?

I need not enter into any detailed answer to the first of these questions. The inspection of the section of a fault in nature will tell more in a few minutes than could be learnt from description in an hour, and the lesson so received will be better remembered. A fault is not usually vertical, but inclined at a high angle. The rocks are commonly somewhat shattered on either side, the central parts of the fracture being filled with the broken rubbish. The breadth of broken material may vary up to a mass of many yards. If, on the face of a cliff, two different sets of rocks are brought together against each other along a steep line of junction, where they are both jumbled and broken, that line will almost certainly be a fault. (Fig. 33.)

The inclination of the sides of the fault is termed its *hade*, and slopes away from the side which has been pushed up, or in the direction of that which has gone down. This is a useful fact, as it enables an observer to note which is the up-throw or down-throw side of a fault. The hade ought therefore always to be noted, and in mining districts its angle of inclination may be conveniently recorded to explain the position of the same dislocation in the underground workings.

Unless the same bed can be recognised on both sides of a fault as exposed in a cliff or other section, it is evident that the fault at that particular place does not reveal the extent of its displacement. It would not in such a case be safe to pronounce the fault to be large or small in the amount of its throw, unless we had other evidence by which to identify the beds on either side. One with a considerable amount of displacement may make little show in a cliff, while on the other hand, one which, to judge from the jumbled and fractured ends of the beds on either side, might be supposed to be a powerful dislocation, may be found to be of comparatively slight importance.   I may cite in illustration, the section exposed on the cliff near Stonehaven in Kincardineshire, where one of the most notable faults in Great

Fig. 33.—Section of a fault.

Britain runs out to sea.   This fault lies between the ancient crystalline rocks of the Highlands and the red sandstones and conglomerates of the Lowlands of Scotland.   So powerful have been its effects that the strata on the Lowland side have been thrown on end for a distance of two miles back from the line of fracture, so as to stand upright along the coast-cliffs, like books on a library shelf.   Yet at the actual point where the fault

reaches the sea and is cut in section by the cliff, it does
not appear as a line of shattered rock.   On the contrary,
no one, placed at once upon the spot, would be likely to
suspect the existence of a fault at all.   The red sandstone and the reddened Highland slates have been so
compressed and, as it were, welded into each other, that
some care is required to trace the demarcation between
them.

Let us consider the nature of the evidence from which
the existence and position of a fault are inferred, though
the actual dislocation itself does not appear in any
exposure of rock.   The upper part of the earth's crust
for a variable depth is traversed by a circulation of water,
which, descending from the surface and performing a
circuitous underground journey, comes out again in the
form of springs.   The divisional planes whereby all
rocks are marked serve as channels along which the
water oozes or flows.   Of these planes none offer such
ready and abundant means of escape to the water as
lines of faults.   Hence in some districts the faults are

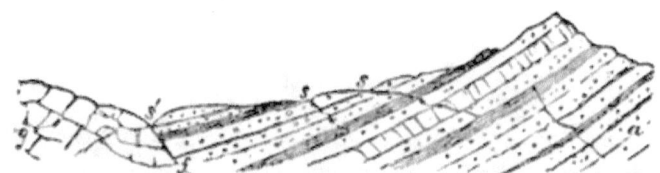

Fig. 34.—Fault marked by the rise of springs at the surface.

traceable at the surface by lines of springs.   Without
some knowledge of the country, we should not indeed be
justified in inferring the existence of a fault merely from
finding a linear series of springs.   These might arise along

the boundary between two different beds or sets of beds
(see Fig. 22).   The springs which issue at the base of the
chalk are an illustration.   But if, having ascertained that
there is no such water-bearing boundary line in the district,
we come upon a marked line of springs, we may surmise
that they indicate the position of a fault, and we may
use them in confirmation of other evidence bearing on
the existence of that fault.   In unravelling the geological
structure of a country, the observer may thus often be
able, by means of springs, to localise a line of fracture,
the existence of which he can demonstrate otherwise.

In the same way, a marked and abrupt change in the
form of the ground along a definite line may serve to

Fig. 35.—Geological section shewing how a prominent feature at the surface
may be caused by the outcrop of a hard rock (*a*) intercalated among softer strata.

show the position of a fault.   It is true that here again
the junction of two beds or two series of rocks of different durability, such as sandstone or limestone upon
clay, or gravels lying against granite, may give rise to a
long straight or curving escarpment or slope.   The mere
existence of such a long line of bank would not of itself
justify any conclusion or inference as to a fault.   In Fig.
35, for example, we see how a steep declivity is produced by the intercalation of a hard bed between
others of a much softer nature.   The underlying strata (*c*)

being more easily worn away have, by their removal,
deprived the thick, solid, overlying mass of its proper
support.   Hence slices of that mass from time to time
slip off and cumber the base of the cliff with ruined
blocks, which tend to arrest the progress of decay until
they themselves are gradually split up by the weather
and removed.   Nevertheless, such abrupt changes of
contour, taken in conjunction with other facts, may often
be made to help in proving the existence of faults.
Marked forms of ground have always some geological
explanation.   It is the province of the field-geologist to
study them in connection with their causes, and to make
use of them in elucidating the structure of the rocks and
the history of the physical geography of a country.

But by far the most important and satisfactory
evidence for the existence and effects of faults is furnished by the grouping of the rocks with reference to
each other, and can only be put together when that
grouping has been examined with some care, in other
words, when some progress has been made in unravelling
the geological structure of the locality.   The nature of this
evidence will be most satisfactorily followed by reference
once more to the map in Figs. 26 and 27.

It will be observed that several lines of fault are
shown upon that map.   Look first at that which crosses
the streams on the left or west side.   In ascending the
most southerly of these streams we notice that at first
the rocks consist of various sedimentary deposits—sandstones, shales, and limestones.   These strata dip toward
the south-east, and the angle gradually rises as we proceed up the stream, until at the last place where they are
seen the beds stand at an angle of 80°.   A short way

higher up we encounter rocks of an entirely different character; let us suppose them to be granite and crystalline metamorphic rocks. The gradual rise of angle and the almost vertical position of the strata would be regarded as sufficient to indicate the existence of a line of fault between the stratified rocks and the crystalline masses. The section in the next stream is similar. It will be observed that while the general order of the strata is the same, some of the beds in the former section do not come out to view here, while, on the other hand, some appear here which were not found before. It is by thus piecing different contiguous sections together that

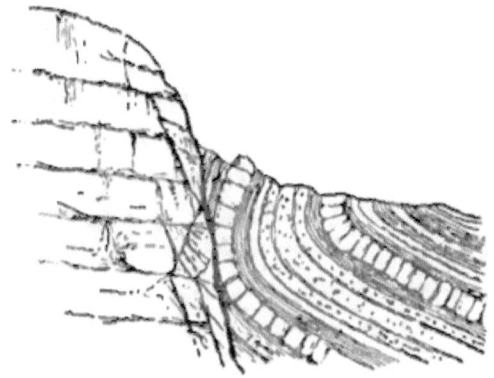

Fig. 36.—Section of fault with inverted beds on the down-throw side.

the order of strata in a district is made out. The angle of dip in this second stream rises as before towards the higher ground inland, until angles of 70° to 80° are reached. It may be remarked that the last rocks seen here lie beyond the line of those last seen in the first stream; also that the obscured space between them and the crystalline masses is narrower. We get deeper into

the series and find that a lower part of it than was seen
before now impinges upon the granitic masses. In the
next stream similar evidence is obtained, only here a little
ambiguity seems at first to arise from the fact that the
strata, after gradually becoming vertical, dip as it were into
or below the granite. This in reality is a reversal of dip.
The strata have not only been thrown on end, but actually
bent back upon themselves, so that a section of them at
that place would show such an arrangement as is given in
Fig. 36. No more convincing evidence of the existence
of a powerful fault could be given. It should be noticed,
too, that here again we have still lower parts of the series
of stratified rocks placed on end against the granitic hills.

Now, having put these various data upon our map, we
see that the point of junction between the two kinds of
rock crosses the streams in a tolerably straight north-
easterly line. There cannot be any doubt that the
junction is a fault; for 1st, there is no trace of any conglomerates or other indications of an original base to the
formation, lying upon and wrapping round the granite ; on
the contrary, the remarkably straight boundary line is not
at all like that of an old shore or unconformable junction ;
2nd, there is no evidence of the granite having been intruded through the rocks. The latter show no granite
veins or traces of alteration.   3rd. The disturbed vertical
and even inverted position of the strata all along the
straight line of junction proves that line to be a fault.
4th. The upturned strata are cut across obliquely by
the junction-line, so that different horizons of them are
successively brought against the crystalline rocks.

We cannot hesitate in such a case to treat the line as
a fault, which we mark on the map by a strong pencil-

Line, at each point where there is good evidence as to its approximate or actual position. We should search for further traces of the line in the intermediate ground; and here may be realised the use of a line of springs, or of some definite bank or hollow on the surface of the ground, in enabling us to carry the line of the fault with confidence across a tract where no actual rock may be exposed. There could be, in the present instance, little hesitation in prolonging our strong pencil-line from point to point; if we felt any uncertainty as to its course through some part of the country, we should make the line there a broken or dotted one.

The side of up-throw or down-throw may either be fixed at once from our knowledge of the order of succession among the rocks, or may be determined at a later stage as our acquaintance with the district increases. Thus, in the case which has just been under notice, if we knew that the granite series was older, that is, underlay the other, we should say that the up-throw of the fault was to the granite side. This direction might be marked on the map by a short bar placed perpendicular to the line of the fault, and on the down-throw side. In the completed map the fault might be shown by a strong black line or by a white line. The latter method is adopted on the maps of the Geological Survey, where fine lines of opaque Chinese-white are placed over the geological colours to mark the position of the faults.

From the example given in the diagram which we have been considering in detail (Fig. 27), it appears that one indication of the proximity of a fault is a rapid rise in the angle of inclination of strata. It is common to find the beds on the down-throw side bent up against the other side, and this upturning may extend for a few feet or for more than a mile.   The amount of disturbance may be regarded as bearing on the whole a relation to the amount of vertical displacement of the fault; though to this conclusion there are many exceptions.   The great fault already referred to as flanking the Scottish Highlands has placed the old red sandstones and conglomerates on end for about two miles.   The beds on the up-throw side, on the other hand, may sometimes be observed to be bent down against the fault.   This arrangement is of course what might have been looked for, but it does not always occur.

Another feature which may be regarded as a tolerably sound proof of the existence of a fault, consists in a complete divergence of strike between the formations on either side of a given line, or, in the common parlance of field-geologists, when one series of strata strikes at or against another.   This may be most easily understood by reference to the diagram (Figs. 26 and 27). Towards the south-east portion of that map, two different sets of strata may be observed to crop up in the various streams and natural sections.   The strike of one of these is at D and C nearly north-west. Towards the north-east, owing to a change in the direction of dip, the strike swings round, until at last it is E.N.E. and W.S.W.   Now, unless some fault occurs, we may confidently expect that the strata which strike north-west and south-east will be found to continue southwards, though they may eventually participate in some other change of strike, and wheel round as before.   If, then, in the line of their strike,

and at a comparatively short distance, in which they
have no room to turn round, we encounter, as shown
here, another and different series of rocks (*F* and *G*),
we may reasonably infer that a fault intervenes, and may
set about the search for further evidence of it.   In the
case supposed upon the map, the strata on the south
side strike on the whole in a north-east and south-west
direction.   But close examination shows that some
strata are cut out as they approach the junction-line ;
this plainly indicates the line to be one of dislocation.

A great many faults run with the dip, and are called
dip-faults ($\phi\phi$ in Fig. 27) ; another series runs with the
strike, forming *strike-faults* ($\phi'\phi'$ in Fig. 27).   But as dislocations may occur in any direction, and cross dip and
strike at any angle, these two series are not very sharply
marked off from, but may pass into each other, or the
same dislocation may be a dip-fault when looked at from
one side, and a strike-fault when viewed from the other
(as at $\phi''\phi''$ and z z in Fig. 27).   Owing to the way in which
denudation has smoothed down the surface of the ground,
a dip-fault has the effect of shifting the outcrop of an inclined stratum so as to make it appear like a horizontal
displacement.   In the map, for example, the beds, *D* and
E dipping south are traversed by a dip-fault with a down-
throw to the east.   The line of outcrop is consequently
shifted northwards on the side of down-throw.   If the
beds had dipped northwards, then a down-throw to the
east would have moved the outcrop southwards.   A
strike-fault, when it exactly coincides with the line of
strike on both sides, makes no change in the line of
outcrop, except in bringing two parallel bands closer
together.   It may carry some important strata out of

K

sight, or prevent them from ever being seen at the
surface at all. In the map (Fig. 27), for example, the bed
C is completely cut out against the strike-fault $\phi'\phi'$. If it
were not seen at the surface elsewhere, its existence could
not be known unless from some underground boring.

To judge of the character and effects of faults upon
the geological structure of a country, the student should
consult some good detailed maps, such as the large coal-
field plans of the Geological Survey of Great Britain. It
is good exercise, too, in the practical treatment of faults
in field-geology, to study some coast-section where the
strata are considerably faulted, and where they are
exposed in plan upon the beach as well as in section
upon the cliff. A river-ravine in summer weather,
when the water is low, sometimes furnishes admirable
lessons in this as well as in other branches of the
subject.

CHAPTER XI.

THE CURVATURE OF ROCKS.

In the limited exposures of strata usually visible, such as those in the bed of a stream, or a sea-shore, in a railway cutting or in a quarry, the planes of dip usually seem in section to be straight lines. Bed succeeds bed inclined at the same angle and forming a succession of parallel bands. But could we continue the sections downward beneath the surface, or see the rocks exposed on the bare steep side of a great mountain, we should observe that though, when examined within the limited area of a few feet or yards, the beds look as if they sloped in straight stiff lines, in reality they are portions of great curves. That this must be so is made evident when we reflect on what must be the consequence of the variations of angle in the inclination of beds at the surface. Suppose, for example, that along the ravine of some river, or in any other natural or artificial opening, we encounter a succession of strata inclined as in Fig. 37. We cannot observe any visible indication of curvature in any of the beds, and yet, if we prolong the planes of dip above and below the surface (Fig. 38) we see at once that there must be a considerable curve, though with a radius so large that the bending does not appear within the narrow strip of

K 2

rock exposed at the surface.   Such indications of endless
undulations in the rocks of the earth's crust meet the
field-geologist at every turn.

FIG. 37.—Section of inclined strata.

The larger curvatures can be best understood from a
previous examination of those on a small scale, so often

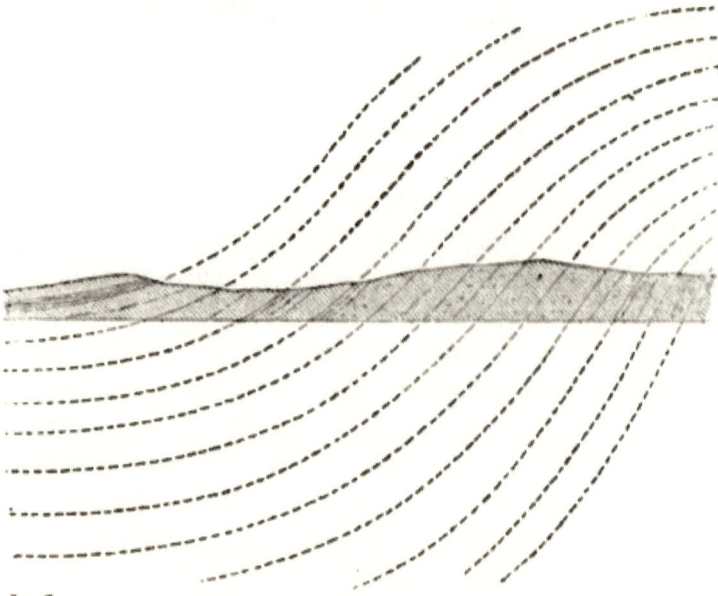

FIG. 38.—Section of inclined strata (as in Fig. 37), showing that they form part
of a large curve.

to be met with on coasts and in inland ravines.   In such
cases we may advance (from say *a* in Fig. 39) across the
strike of beds dipping steadily towards us, and may not,

from all that appears, suspect that any marked fold of the rocks is contained in the section. And yet on reaching *b* we should at once perceive that we were standing on the centre of an arch, saddle, or anticline, and that if we went on towards *c* we must cross the same strata over again. Or, on the other hand, were we to

FIG. 39.—Section of strata curved in an arch or Anticline.

traverse a succession of strata dipping continuously away from us, as from *a* to *b* in Fig. 40, and to come at last to a flattening of them and the commencement of a dip in the opposite direction, we should know that in this case the rocks had been folded into a basin, trough, or syncline.

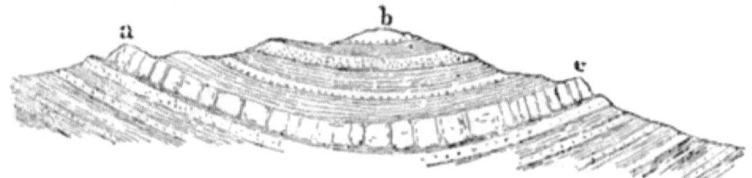

FIG. 40.—Section of strata curved in a trough or Syncline.

The concealment of the central portion or axis of the fold where, on a small scale, as in the cases I have supposed, the actual bending of the rocks may be seen, does not make any difference in the interpretation to be put upon the contrary dips at *a* and *c* in Figs. 39 and 40. Indeed, in nature it is comparatively rare to see the actual

central bending of the strata.   In almost all cases,
except the minor examples I have spoken of, the line of
axis is determined from the angles taken among the inclined
strata on either side.   And here the advantage of one
or more definite horizons is made strikingly apparent.
If we can recognise the same stratum on both sides of a
fold, we have in its position and angle of inclination
a datum line from which to measure the extent of the
fold.   In Fig. 39, for example, if the bed marked *a c*
can be identified on each side of the arch, we can estimate from the angles of inclination between it and the
axis how high the arch must have been when this bed
formed its crown, and what amount of material has
since been removed.   On the other hand it is easy
in a similar way to calculate the depth of the trough
(Fig. 40) from the centre down to the position of the
stratum *a, c.*

We might expect that these curvatures of the solid
rocks should always produce features at the surface, that
the lines of anticlinal axis should correspond with ridges
or hills, and that those of synclinal folds should define
the trend of valleys.   But it often, perhaps we may even
say generally, happens that neither anticlines nor synclines
produce any marked influence on the surface (Fig. 42).
In walking over the two sections (Figs. 39 and 40), the
observer not attending to the angles of inclination, would
never suspect that he was crossing a geological ridge in
the one case, and a geological valley in the other.   When
these curvatures affect the contour of the surface, they
are apt to do so exactly in the opposite way to that
which the learner might have anticipated.   The anticlinal
folds not unusually coincide with, and have given rise

to, lines of valley; while the synclinal folds have origin-
ated lines of ridge or hill.

FIG. 41.—Anticlines forming valleys; synclines forming hills.

But the observer as he extends his experience will find
that not only have the rocks of the earth's crust been

FIG. 42.—Curved limestone, Draughton, near Skipton.

folded in this equable and gentle way; but that they
present proofs of much more intense movement. These

.may be looked for in the vicinity of faults, as has already been pointed out. Sudden and violent crumpling in the midst of comparatively undisturbed strata may be regarded as *primâ facie* indicative of the proximity of some dislocation. It will not however of itself be sufficient to prove the existence of a fault, for unexpected

FIG. 43.—Shales contorted by a landslip.

local twists and severe plication sometimes occur where, though the rocks must have been subjected to intense lateral compression, they have not actually been fractured. On a small scale the most tumultuous contortion of soft strata may often be seen as the result of a landslip. In Fig. 43, for example, a set of dark shales lying under a

thick sandstone have been crushed up by slips of the
heavy over-lying rock, yet the ruin has been so well concealed by vegetation that a careless observer might suppose the lower twisted beds to be much older than, and
unconformably covered by, the upper horizontal strata.

There occur wide tracts of country where the underlying rocks have been so violently disturbed, that for miles
they seem to be standing on end. In such cases it is
usual to find some one prevalent direction of strike along
which the vertical or highly inclined beds range themselves. And a careful examination will generally disclose

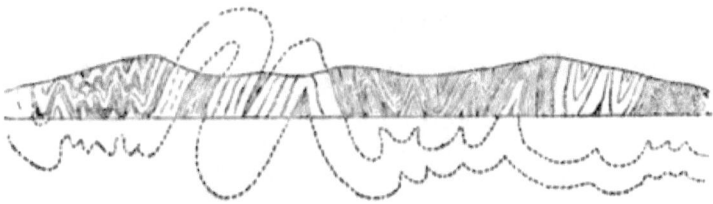

Fig. 44.—Section of what at the surface might be mistaken for a continuous
highly inclined series of strata, shown to consist of numerous anticlinal and
synclinal folds. Gneissose rocks, Lock Quoich, Invernesshire.

proofs that the strata really consist of many rapid folds,
the same beds being repeated again and again. Subsequent extensive denudation has worn away the tops of
the arches and produced a form of surface which may
have little or no reference to the structure of the rocks
below (Fig. 44).

Rocks contorted in this way are pretty sure to present
cases of *isoclinal* folds, that is, the axes of the curves are
not vertical but inclined. In Fig. 45, for example, the
folds are all inclined in the same direction, so that in
each of them one half of the curve has its strata turned

bottom uppermost. Inversions on a grand scale are to be seen in great mountain-chains like the Alps. The accompanying drawing (Fig. 46) represents a very remarkable example which occurs in the mass of the Glärnisch, one of the eastern Swiss Alps, as described by Dr.

FIG. 45.—Inverted contortions or isoclinal folds.

Baltzer. The peak (Ruchen) reaches a height of 2,107 metres above the valley to the left of it (Klönthal). The folded rocks belong to the Cretaceous system of the Alps.

FIG. 46.—Section of the grand inversions of strata in the Glärnisch Mountain, Eastern Alps.

Cleavage.—By the powerful lateral pressure to which rocks have been subjected during their subsidence and contortion, their minute particles, which usually present one axis longer than the others, have been compelled to adjust themselves in the rock along the

line of least resistance ; that is, with their longer axis
perpendicular to the direction of the pressure. Mr.
Sorby showed by ingenious experiments, that with
suitable adjustments of pressure this re-arrangement
could be imitated artificially in different substances,
even in so homogeneous a body as wax poured in a
melted state upon a surface of glass. Rocks in which
the change has been superinduced are said to be cleaved,
and the change itself is termed cleavage.

Considerable practice is required to be able to distinguish between the fissile structure thus developed by
cleavage, and that due to original lamination of deposit.
Should the rock consist of alternate bands of different
textures, such alternation will of itself be sufficient to
show the bedding ; while a further test will be found
in the frequent difference in the fineness of the cleavage
as it passes from one rock into another. Fine-grained
argillaceous rocks assume the most perfect cleavage ;
hence their value as slates. Sandy and gritty rocks
do not allow of the development of such fine divisional
planes. Consequently the cleavage lines may actually
be seen to stop when they reach an arenaceous stratum
and begin again on the further side at the next argillaceous
band. Where no such intercalation of different strata can
be observed, the geologist looks for lines of colour
corresponding with original lamination. Should these
fail, he may for an interval find it impossible to make
sure in what direction the lines of stratification run. It
will be perceived from Fig. 47 that cleavage runs independent of original bedding, coinciding with it or
not, as the strata may happen to lie. The strike of the
cleavage which can be traced with great persistence over

large areas, as in North Wales, marks the direction
perpendicular to which the compression of the rocks
took place.   In following it, therefore, the observer

FIG. 47.—Cleavage of curved strata, coinciding with the stratification at *b b*, but
at a right angle to it at *a*.

will keep a watch for every indication of other evidence
as to the nature and extent of the terrestrial movements
by which these great changes were effected.

CHAPTER XII.

THE foregoing chapters have treated chiefly of the structure of the stratified rocks, although the same principles which guide us in dealing with them are also in great part applicable to the igneous rocks. These latter, however, present some features of their own which mark them off in strong contrast with the former, and which the geologist can learn to distinguish only by actual practice in the field.

At the outset, the observer must be able to recognise an igneous rock when he meets with it. In the great majority of cases he will have no difficulty in this, provided he has made himself familiar with the characters of such rocks by handling specimens of them. But the carefully selected specimens of a museum or private collection do not always convey a correct idea of the external character of the rocks as they occur on the hillside or ravine. It is specially needful that the hammer be vigorously plied during at least the earlier part of a geologist's study of igneous rocks. He will find them so constantly decayed at the surface, so thickly covered with a weathered crust, and even, in many cases, so deeply

penetrated by the percolating water which has decomposed their silicates, that he may experience no little
difficulty in procuring a tolerably fresh fracture from
which to judge what the real character of the rock may
be.   The weathered surface, however, often helps in this
discrimination, for the decay of the more decomposable
mineral sometimes leaves the others more easily recognisable than in the unaltered state.   Should the observer
find himself at a loss how to name a rock, let him take
one or two chips in his pocket, wrapping them in paper,
with a label inside, to mark their proper locality.   When
he gets back to his quarters in the evening he may submit
one or two minute splinters of the rock to blow-pipe
tests, or if these be inapplicable, or give no satisfactory
results, he may proceed, in the manner described in a
later chapter, to prepare a slice of the stone, mount it
on glass, and submit it to examination under the microscope.   If even after all these trials the rock still puzzles
him, he had better give it some provisional name, and
lose no more time over its determination, but proceed with his field-work, laying aside, however, some
good typical specimens of the doubtful rock for subsequent more careful analysis either by himself or some
experienced petrographer.

Having acquired more or less facility in detecting
igneous rocks by their lithological characters, the observer
may proceed to study their structures as rock-masses and
the part they have played in the architecture of the earth's
crust.   He will find by practice that for the purposes of
field-geology they are conveniently divisible into two great
series—(1) the Crystalline, including granite, syenite, with
all the once melted rocks like the lavas; and (2) the

Fragmental, including the consolidated volcanic ashes, tuffs, and conglomerates. As a rule, these two series are broadly and distinctly marked off from each other, both by lithological character and by their behaviour as rock-masses. The crystalline rocks, as their name indicates, have solidified from molten or aquo-igneous solutions ; sometimes remaining still in their condition of glass, sometimes completely crystalline and with every possible gradation between these two extremes. But though tor the most part recognisably crystalline in the field, they are not always so. Many ancient porphyries for example might in hand-specimens be taken for pieces of hardened clay. In such cases, should the lithological characters be indefinite, the true character of the rock may usually be ascertained from its relation to the surrounding masses. If these are obscured, the final appeal may be to the microscope. Hence the learner must be prepared for endless varieties of texture, colour, hardness and soft-ness, toughness and friableness, among the once molten igneous rocks. The fragmental series is less varied, as the rocks belonging to it consist of fragmentary ma-terials, derived partly from the explosion of lava rising in the throats of volcanoes, and partly from the *débris* torn from the sides of the volcanic funnels and craters. They are essentially characterised by the fragmental or "clastic" nature of their component particles. These may vary in texture from the finest impalpable dust up to blocks weighing several tons. Hence considerable variety exists in the coarseness or fineness of the con-solidated strata. They may pass on the one hand by admixture of ordinary sediment into sandstones and shales ; on the other, into the coarse tumultuous agglo-

merate of purely volcanic origin so commonly found
filling up former vents of eruption.

The Crystalline igneous rocks may be conveniently
classed as deep-seated or plutonic, and as superficial or
volcanic, according as they have solidified deep within
the crust, or at or near the surface, though fundamentally
they are all parts of one great series.   In the more superficial or volcanic group, these rocks may either be intrusive
or interbedded ; that is, they may either have been intruded among the rocks with which they are associated,

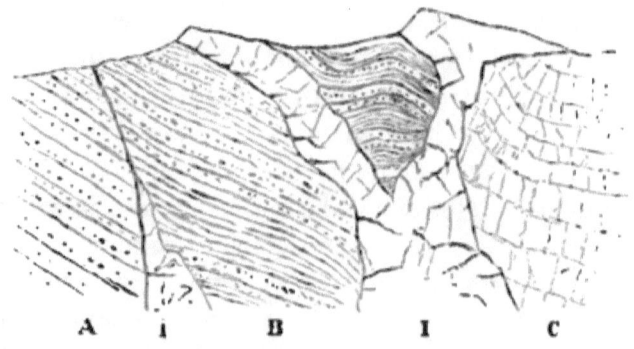

A   i   B   I   C

Fig. 48.—Section of a portion of the earth's crust broken by two dislocations
whereby three different masses of stratified rock, A. B. and C, have been
brought into juxtaposition, and with two masses of intrusive igneous rock
I, which have risen along the lines of fracture.

or they may have been poured out at the surface in sheets,
which in a great continuous series of deposits thus come
to be interbedded between the strata below and those
above them.   It is of course evident that as these crystalline masses have all risen from molten reservoirs
below, they were all originally intrusive in the earlier or
deeper part of their course.   Every interbedded sheet
must have been connected somewhere underneath with
the intrusive pipe or vein by which it rose to the surface,

although the connection may have been subsequently destroyed or concealed. An intrusive mass, on the other hand, may never have been connected with the surface at all. Interbedded igneous rocks prove the former existence of active volcanic vents at or near the localities in which they occur. Intrusive igneous rocks may be due to ancient deep - seated movements in the crust of the earth which never gave rise to any of those surface manifestations usually held to be expressed by the term volcanic. An accurate discrimination between these two groups is of importance when the history of a volcanic district has to be made out.

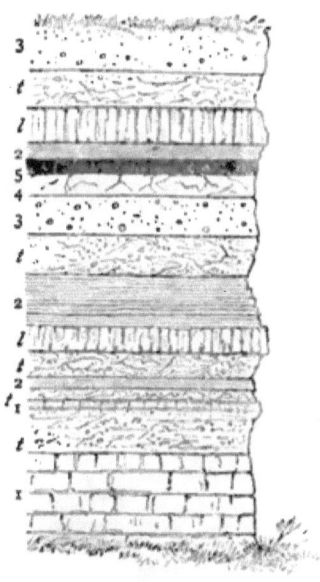

FIG. 49. — Section of interbedded igneous rocks, Linlithgowshire. *l, l,* lavas; *t, t,* tuffs; 1, limestone with marine organisms; 2, shale; 3, sandstone; 4, fire-clay; 5, coal.

1. I may briefly notice some of the main characters which distinguish the groups. An intrusive rock may occur in the form of (1) a vein (*v* in Fig. 52), traversing at any angle the rocks among which it lies, (2) a vertical wall-like mass or dyke, (3) an irregularly circular boss forming the upper end of a vertical column or pipe called a "neck," (4) an injected bed or sheet (*b*, Fig. 52), or (5) an irregular amorphous mass. When it can be seen to intersect any of the beds of a series of strata, its intrusive character becomes at once apparent. But when it lies between stratified rocks, and

L

assumes the form of a bed, some care is needed to make its intrusive character certain, for it might then be taken for an interbedded sheet.   It is usually characterised by

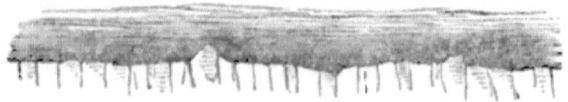

FIG. 50.—Upper surface of an intrusive igneous sheet with overlying shale.

being much closer in grain near its junction with the other rocks than in the central parts of its mass (Fig. 50). Again the rocks lying upon it are hardened, and some-

FIG. 51.—View of the Island of Staffa and Fingal's Cave, showing amorphous and columnar basalt resting upon tuff.

times exceedingly altered, while detached portions of them are now and then found to have been caught up and entangled in the crystalline mass below.

The position of the prismatic joints by which volcanic rocks are frequently traversed may sometimes suffice to indicate whether a rock is certainly intrusive or, possibly, interbedded. These joints start from the cooling surfaces of the original melted mass of lava. In a bed they are of course perpendicular to its upper and under surfaces (Fig. 51) ; in a dyke or vein they vary according to the inclination of the mass, being horizontal when the dyke is vertical (Fig. 52).

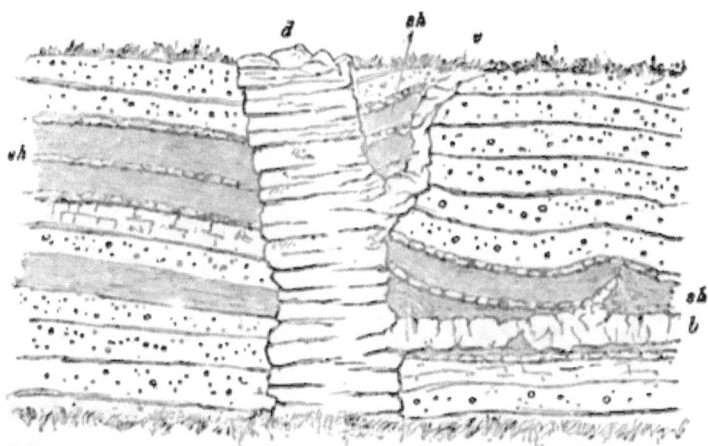

Fig. 52.—Section of a dyke (*d*), rising through a small fault and sending out a vein (*v*), and an intrusive sheet or bed (*b*), into the surrounding shales and iron stones (*sh*).

When an igneous rock has been cut through by a fault, the fractured surface, especially when rough and shattered, may assume a deceptive resemblance to the side of a truly intrusive mass. But in such a case it would probably be found that the surfaces both of the igneous rock and of those next it showed, in their striated and polished appearance, evidence of having been made to grind each other as solid masses.

Dykes vary in thickness from less than an inch to seventy feet or more, and from a vertical to a steeply-inclined position. They often rise along previous lines of fracture ; but in the great majority of cases the basalt-dykes of Tertiary date, so abundant in Britain, have filled fissures without any vertical throw of the rocks on either side. Sometimes a dyke may be found, as in Fig. 52, to send out ramifications, though this is not so common as might be supposed.

The amount of alteration on the surrounding rock produced by dykes is usually surprisingly small. Sandstone is hardened into a kind of quartzite, and occasionally even acquires a columnar structure, the prisms being directed outwards from the sides of the dyke. But the alteration seldom exceeds a few feet. Shales suffer more, as they are found baked into a kind of porcelain-jasper; but this may frequently be observed not to extend more than an inch or two into the rock ; while along many dykes the shales show scarcely any perceptible hardening. It is where they come in contact with carbonaceous shales, or still more with seams of coal, that dykes and intrusive sheets produce their most marked metamorphism. The coal has sometimes been entirely consumed, and a layer of igneous rock has taken its place. At other times a thin sheet of molten lava has been injected along the top, bottom, or centre of the coal-seam, converting it into a kind of anthracite or a mere cinder. Examples may be found where the coal has been fused into a cellular mass, and has subsequently had its vesicles filled up with infiltrated

carbonate of lime.   In Ayrshire numerous beautiful
sections have been laid bare, where the coal has been
rendered prismatic, the hexagonal or polygonal prisms,
like so many bundles of pencils, diverging from the surface of the intruded igneous rock.   At the same time
it is where they have inflicted such injury upon coals and
carbonaceous shales, that the igneous masses have themselves experienced most alteration.   The most solid
black crystalline basalt, where it runs through one of these
strata is changed into a pale dull yellow or white clay, so
deceptively like some of the fire-clays of the coal-fields
that it will hardly be admitted by most observers to be
anything else until they trace out its relations.   But they
may find it passing insensibly into the ordinary condition
of basalt, as it recedes from the carbonaceous bed the
combustion of which had reduced its oxides.   A thin section of one of these "white rocks," placed under the microscope, still shows traces of the original structure of the
basalt, but with the component minerals entirely altered.

It would seem that, as a rule, the extent of alteration
in the rocks adjoining an intrusive igneous mass bears
some proportion to the size of the latter.   We may be
prepared for traces of the change at a greater distance
from a large injected sheet than from a small dyke.

The "necks" which mark the sites of former volcanic funnels are filled up sometimes with crystalline
rocks, sometimes with tuff or coarse agglomerate.   They
descend, of course, vertically through the surrounding
rocks, which are sometimes considerably altered all
round.   They vary in size from a few yards to a
mile or more in diameter.   Many interesting examples
have been mapped in the course of the Geological

Survey of Scotland, in the Old Red Sandstone, Carbon
iferous, and Permian system.

2. Interbedded igneous rocks are sheets of volcanic material which have been ejected at the surface and have
solidified there. Consequently, whenever they can be
satisfactorily determined, they show the former existence
of volcanic activity on or near to their site. The geological
date of their eruption can be ascertained by an examination of the strata with which they have been contemporaneously associated. Thus, for instance, if we find a
set of lavas and tuffs interstratified with limestones and
shales containing *Productus giganteus, Lingula squami-
formis, Athyris ambigua, Lithostrotion junceum,* &c., we
conclude without hesitation that as these are unequivo-
cally Carboniferous Limestone fossils, the volcanic
eruptions must have taken place during the period of
the Carboniferous Limestone.

It is important therefore to be able to determine satisfactorily whether or not a group of igneous rocks has been
contemporaneously poured out during the deposition of
the formation in which they occur, or has been injected
into that formation probably at a comparatively recent
date. The existence of unmistakable beds of tuff would
settle the question. These rocks consist of ejected
volcanic detritus, and must have been laid down at the
surface ; they could not be injected as in the case of
crystalline rocks. Whenever, therefore, we encounter
interstratifications of volcanic tuff in a group of sedimentary formations, we are justified in regarding them as
evidence of contemporaneous volcanic activity.

But the proof is vastly strengthened when we find not
only the consolidated volcanic ashes, but also the lava-

streams of the period. A truly interbedded sheet of crystalline rock is, in fact, a lava-stream which has been poured out at the surface, either on land or under water, and shows the distinctive characters of such a bed, Thus it is commonly rough and slag-like towards its top and bottom, and most compact about the centre. The beds lying upon it, having been deposited there after the emission of the lava, are not altered, have no portions of their strata entangled in the crystalline rock, but, on the contrary, may contain detached fragments of the latter.

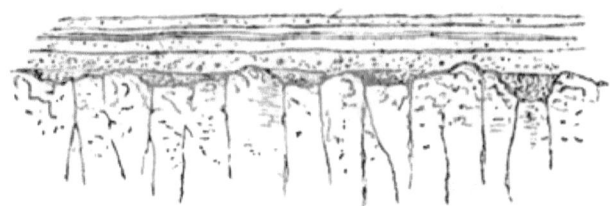

Fig. 53.—Upper surface of an interbedded igneous sheet with sedimentary strata lying upon it.

It is eminently characteristic of lava to acquire a cellular texture, from the expansion of the abundant steam imprisoned within it at the time of eruption. This feature is specially developed at the top where, the pressure being least, the vapour has had most freedom of motion. As the vesicles appeared while the rock continued to move, they may frequently be observed to be pulled out into oval or almond shapes (*amygdaloidal*) in the direction of the motion (Fig. 54). Indications of this kind mark the flow of lavas in all geological periods, and should always be noted when they occur.

The upper part of a lava-stream still in motion is often a confused heap of rough blocks of slag, among which rents appear opening down into the still red-hot mass underneath.   Many of these rents remain unclosed when the lava comes to rest.   If we imagine such a cracked sheet of rock to have sand or mud laid over its surface, the cracks would certainly be filled up first, and if the sand were brought in gradually, there might be time for it to arrange itself in a stratified manner between the walls of the fissures.   No better evidence could be given that the lava must have been poured out at the surface,

FIG. 54.—Steam-holes in lava drawn out in the direction of the flow of the mass (e f.) and becoming more and more flattened till on the line a b they are compressed into mere streaks and give a fissile structure to the rock.

and not injected as an intrusive sheet.   Evidence of this nature abounds in many parts of the volcanic rocks of the Old Red Sandstone of Scotland (Fig. 55).

In these examples the lava was succeeded by a period of volcanic quiescence, during which ordinary sediment was washed over its surface.   Sometimes the lava-beds in an old geological formation are succeeded by beds of volcanic tuff, or these two kinds of rock are intercalated with each other in such a way as to show that streams of lava and showers of dust and stones must have been erupted too rapidly to permit of the accumulation of any prominent beds of ordinary sediment between them.   The

way in which lavas and tuffs sometimes alternate in a
series of ancient strata is well illustrated in Fig. 49, which
represents the characteristic grouping of volcanic and
sedimentary materials in the Carboniferous Limestone
series of Linlithgowshire.   In the diagram, Fig. 27, the
series of rocks marked *P* in the southern part of the
map are examples of interbedded lavas and tuffs.   They

FIG. 55.—Cracks in an Old Red Sandstone lava which have been filled in with
sandstone from above, Coast of Kincardineshire.

occur under circumstances very similar to those of ordinary stratified rocks.   They dip one below the other in
orderly succession, and are traversed by faults, like the
beds of sandstone and conglomerate which lie below,
between, and above them.   In an actual volcanic cone,
where only volcanic materials occur, a more complex
arrangement is found.   Lavas and tuffs there succeed
each other in rapid alternations, often cut by dykes or

veins. Instances are comparatively rare where cones belonging to old geological periods have been preserved. It is not uncommon, however, to meet with the "necks" above described, which may be regarded as the roots or stumps of cones from which the overlying pile of ejected materials has been worn away by denudation (V V in Fig. 27). This lower or downward prolongation of the original cone, as I have already mentioned, may consist either of masses of lava or other crystalline rock, or of consolidated fragmentary materials. In the latter case the tuff or agglomerate has sometimes become itself crystalline, owing, no doubt, to the long continued upward passage of steam, hot vapours, and gases through the volcanic vent after the explosions ceased.

As illustrations of the way in which the structure of a volcanic region is worked out and expressed upon a map, I may refer to the sheets of the Geological Survey of England and Wales, particularly 75 and 78, embracing the Snowdon region; and to sheets 22, 23, 32, 33, and 40 of the Geological Survey of Scotland, showing the development of the volcanoes of the Old Red Sandstone, Carboniferous, and Permian periods in the midland districts of Scotland.

The deep-seated or plutonic rocks include granite and the massive rocks associated intrusively with the crystalline schists. They contain, of course, no true fragmental series. They have no cellular, scoriform portions, which could only be formed towards the surface, where by relief from pressure, the imprisoned steam had liberty to expand and push aside the particles of the still fluid rock. Having cooled slowly under great pressure, they are often highly crystalline. They occur as huge amorphous

masses, sometimes seventy miles long, as in the granite
of the south-east of Ireland. They also assume the
form of veins and dykes, often ramifying in the most
complex way through the rocks which they traverse.

These features can be well studied round the flanks of
a large mass of granite (Fig. 56). A network of veins
may sometimes be seen proceeding from the granite,
intersecting each other and inclosing portions of the
surrounding rock. The veins vary from a breadth of
many yards down to the merest thread. A marked variation in lithological character may be observed as a rule
to attend these changes in the dimensions of the veins.

FIG. 56 —Granite veins, Cornwall. (De la Beche.)

The larger veins may consist of crystalline granite, like
that of the main mass ; but as they ramify and diminish
they pass into an elvanite or fine-grained felsite. Round
the flanks of a granitic mass the sedimentary strata
are found to be much altered, passing even into crystalline schists. The breadth of metamorphosed rock
often exceeds a mile.

CHAPTER XIII.

A GEOLOGIST who, with some little experience of stratified and igneous rocks, finds himself for the first time in
a region of gneiss and schist, meets on every hand with
phenomena, which, though he may be familiar enough
with the descriptions of them in books, cannot but
strike him as strangely anomalous when he comes
actually face to face with them in nature. The rocks
are certainly crystalline, and in small fragments or
hand-specimens may often recall some of the igneous
rocks with which he may already be acquainted. But
when he looks at them in mass they have an arrangement of their component minerals such as he never observed in any igneous rock. The felspars, hornblende,
quartz, mica, and other abundant minerals, are disposed in
more or less regular wavy lines, and the rock splits along
these lines more readily than in other directions. Again,
so distinct sometimes are the parallel seams of different
mineral composition, that the rocks might at first be
mistaken for ordinary sedimentary strata. Yet a little
further examination shows that the layers or folia are
welded or felted into each other by the interweaving of

their crystalline constituents, that they are usually very
inconstant, that they are apt to thicken out capriciously
into concretions and thin away rapidly, and that they
often possess a curious puckered or crumpled character, which can be seen in large contortions on the face of
a mountain, and descends even into such minute forms
as can only be observed with a microscope. It is evident
that rocks presenting such remarkable characters must
offer many points of difficulty as well as of interest to the
field-geologist.

In beginning the examination of a region of foliated
rocks, the observer may of course dismiss from his mind
the idea of receiving help from organic remains. In rare
instances indeed traces of fossils have been obtained from
schistose rocks, or from altered limestones associated with
these rocks. But this is an accident not to be counted
upon. With the absence of palæontological assistance
there is also a great lack of stratigraphical aids, so that the
learner may be led, after a few efforts, to give up as hopelessly impracticable the task of making out any structure of
the ground. Yet he will be surprised in the end with what
can be done by patiently observing the puzzling masses.
He may be led to collect their minerals, and if so, will find
them in many places, particularly among the limestones,
to be a rich storehouse of beautiful and interesting varieties.
By degrees he will discover that particular rocks are distinguishable by special minerals, and he may even be able
to trace such rocks or bands of rock across the mountains
by means of these peculiar minerals, which will thus be
put to the same kind of use as fossils are by the strati-
grapher. Gradually the idea of following the same band
among the contorted masses of the schistose rocks will

seem to him more and more feasible; and he may at
length be induced seriously to make the attempt to
unravel the complicated geological structure of the
region.

In these investigations I have found that four points
deserve to be kept steadily in view.   1. The nature and
distribution of the minerals.   2. The varieties, distribution, and alternations of the rocks.   3. The direction of
the prevalent foliation.   4. The position of the axes of
contortion, and the dip of the rocks from them.

1. As I have just said, the minerals for which regions
of gneiss and schist are celebrated may be employed by
the stratigraphical geologist much as he would use fossils.
Of course they have a far wider meaning than this.
Besides their own beauty, they afford endless interest
and instruction in the light they cast upon the formation
of the rocks among which they occur, and in the problems
they present to us regarding mineral growth. But these
aspects must be studied chiefly in the laboratory, and
with the microscope.   In field-geology, the observer
notes as many facts as strike his mind in connection with
theoretical speculation, but for his own work at the time
it is the association and distribution of the minerals
which are of prime importance.   He will therefore watch,
as he traverses the mountains, under what circumstances
special minerals occur.   Let us suppose for example, that
he encounters a rock containing the beautiful blueish-
grey mineral called kyanite.   He carefully notes how it
occurs, with what other minerals associated, and in what
kind of rock.   Wherever he comes upon a fragment of
the mineral he tries to find it *in situ*, and if successful,
compares the new habitat with those previously observed.

Let us further assume that he discovers it always to lie in the same long-bladed plates or prisms, with the same associated group of minerals, and in the same or a similar kind of rock.   This fact established would be one of high importance in any attempt to work out the geological structure of the district.   In many wide regions, however, no such special mineral zones are to be seen.   The rocks possess a singular monotony of character, or their abundant minerals are not confined to special horizons, so that if their order is to be determined, it must be done by some other method than that furnished by mineral evidence.

2. But where the rocks furnish no specially prominent mineral zones, they often present in themselves great varieties of composition, structure, and texture.   The observer will duly note these characters in connection with their bearing upon the history of the rocks.   He will also try to ascertain whether they have any persistence, and can be utilised as helps towards understanding the arrangement of the rock-masses.   For example, he discovers, let us suppose, a coarse-grained mass of gneiss with large crystals of pink orthoclase—so peculiar a rock that even small fragments can readily be recognised. After examining its lithological characters, he proceeds to investigate its surroundings.   He finds that though, when looked at in detail, it seems structureless, like a coarsely crystallized granite, yet that a distinct foliated structure exists throughout its mass, and that parallel with this foliation there occur, on either side, bands of a different composition, such as folia of hornblende and quartz, or of felspar and mica, or of some other combination of the same or other minerals, sufficient to mark off these

bands from the gneiss. Hence the gneiss itself is a
thick bed or bed-like mass, and its continuation must be
traced along, and not across, the line of foliation. If it
can be followed from point to point for some distance,
its outcrop will become a line or horizon from which to
work out the structure, and estimate the thickness of the
rocks of the district.

Bands of limestone are particularly valuable as guides
in unravelling the structure of a schistose country. Their
line of outcrop can frequently be followed even from a
distance by the track of brighter green herbage, supported
by the richer calcareous soil which they yield, and con-
trasting sometimes strongly with the brown moorland on
either side. In a cultivated region, especially where the
surface is obscured by superficial accumulations, quarries
may often be found in the limestone, admitting of an
inspection of its character and mineral contents. Limestone bands, moreover, among schistose, as among
ordinary sedimentary strata, are not infrequently distinguished by their continuity.

Each district must be judged of by itself, and according
to its local peculiarities will be the choice of zones by
the geologist. He will endeavour to ascertain in what
order the different varieties of rock succeed each other,
whether or not in any continuous section he can determine an order of succession among them, and whether if
such an order can be made out in one place, it can be
extended to others.

3. Apart from the constant variations in the lithological
nature of the rocks, it is desirable to observe whether
there is any persistent strike in the foliation. Over
large tracts of the Highlands of Scotland, the direction of

the foliation of the schists is as persistent, constant, and
easily traced as the strike of any series of sedimentary
formations.   On the other hand, variations in the line of
strike will be noted, if possible on a map, that their
bearing on the geological structure of the ground may
be eventually ascertained.

4. All foliated rocks present, with greater or less
prominence, proofs of having been intensely compressed.
Sometimes they appear to be ranged vertically, like
books in a library.   But a long line of bedded rocks set
on end means, as we have already seen, that they have
been folded upon themselves, and that the tops of the
folds have been cut away. (See p. 137, Fig. 44.)   If it is
difficult to follow out the structure of a crumpled region
of ordinary sedimentary rocks, it is tenfold more arduous
to make progress in one of the crystalline schists.   The
observer, however, may do much by making numerous
and careful observations of the direction and angle of dip,
where he finds that the folia are not vertical.   In this
way he may detect lines of anticlinal and synclinal
axes, and if he be fortunate enough to meet with
any recognisable bands among the rocks, he may, by
tracing them in their successive outcrops on different
sides of these axes, succeed in deciphering the geological structure of the area.   I have used this method
with success among the greatly contorted schists of the
Scottish Highlands.

Every fact which can throw light upon the circumstances in which the foliated rocks were produced
deserves the careful attention of the geologist in the
field.   It is often possible, for instance, to trace among
the arenaceous members of the series relics of the false

M

bedding so characteristic of ordinary sandstones. Many schists are interleaved with bands of grit full of water-worn pebbles of different materials. Even bands of conglomerates may be traced among them. These and similar data go to prove that the rocks were originally sedimentary strata, and that their peculiar foliated structure has been superinduced upon them over wide regions, as it has been upon similar rocks in the metamorphosed band round masses of granite. Foliation or the crystallization of

FIG. 57.—Foliation of mica-schist and grit-bands, coincident with bedding.

mineral aggregates in definite laminæ must have taken place along the dominant divisional planes of the rock. In the great majority of cases these planes would doubtless be those of original stratification. The coincidence between the direction of foliation and stratification is well brought out by the sharply-defined bands of hardened sandstone, grit, conglomerate, &c., which divide many masses of schist exactly as they might do masses of shale (Fig. 57).

MINERAL VEINS.

In connection with the schistose rocks I may refer to mineral veins which so often traverse these masses, though also found abundantly among stratified formations, and even in igneous rocks. Like lines of fault, with which indeed they often coincide, mineral veins, that is, veins filled with segregated minerals of various kinds different from the surrounding rock, do not in the majority of cases appear at the surface. Their existence must be determined from other evidence, therefore, than actual visible sections of them. If the geologist is at work in a district where veins of this kind occur, he should endeavour as early as possible to make himself familiar with the characteristic mineral substances which may constitute the chief part of the veins. Such minerals as quartz, barytes, calcite, and other "veinstones," as they are called, are of common occurrence, but often exhibit local peculiarities by which they may be recognised and traced to their sources. Having examined sections of some of the mineral veins, and learnt the way in which the vein-stones are associated with any metalliferous ore, the observer may be on the watch for evidence of the occurrence of the veins elsewhere. He follows with this view the same plan as that which I have already described with reference to the tracing of the limits of formations by means of scattered surface fragments. In ascending a stream or a hill-side, he takes note of any marked number of pieces of vein-stone, and of the point beyond which they grow fewer or cease. Having thus got a rough indication of the existence of one or more veins, he proceeds to a more minute search

over that part of the ground, and unless the rocks should
be too much concealed, he may hope to meet with an
indication of the actual outcrop of the vein.   It is not
always, nor perhaps often, safe to pronounce as to the

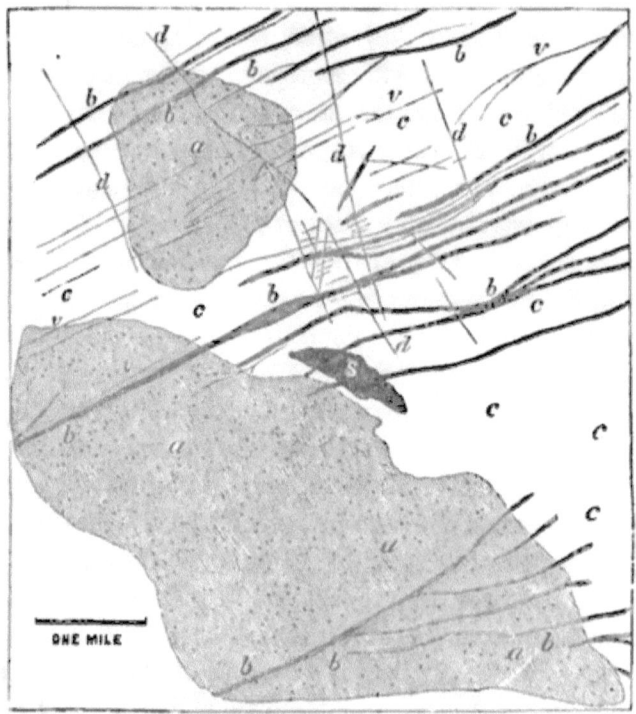

ONE MILE

FIG. 58.—Map of part of the mining district of Gwennap, Cornwall. *aa*, granite;
cc, the surrounding schistose rocks; *bb*, elvan dykes; *s*, "greenstone;"
vv and *dd*, two sets of metalliferous veins, or lodes and cross-courses. (De
la Beche's *Geological Observer*, p. 566.)

commercial value of such a vein from surface evidence
of this kind.   The rock may need to be opened up, and
boring or mining may be required for some way below the

surface before a reliable opinion can be expressed as to whether or not the vein may be worked to profit.

Mineral veins commonly run in straight or slightly bent lines, and often may be grouped in two or more series, one of which is usually cut by the others, forming thus a network of main-veins and cross-veins. The disposition of these veins may be inferred from the accompanying map of a portion of one of the mineral tracts of Cornwall (Fig. 58). The metalliferous character of a vein is apt to vary with the nature of the rock ; plenty of ore may be obtained so long as the vein runs in one rock, but the supply is apt to diminish, or even to die out altogether in another rock.

CHAPTER XIV.

SURFACE GEOLOGY.

In the foregoing pages we have been dealing almost entirely with the solid rocks, their structure and behaviour as constituent portions of the earth's crust. Allusions have been made to their superficial aspects and to the loose accumulations of various kinds by which they are so often concealed. In this chapter let us look cursorily at a few of the aspects of what is sometimes called "surface geology."

And first, of the influence of the solid rocks upon the surface. The distinctive characters imparted by some rocks to scenery have already been referred to.[1] Sometimes it is a question of relative durability. The chalk escarpment in the south of England, for example, stands out so prominently because it is underlaid by more easily degraded sands. Certain portions of a rock may rise high above the rest because of some particular power of resistance they may happen to possess. But one leading influence in the gradual degradation of all rocks is supplied by their *joints*. Every one who has looked into a quarry or railway-cutting, or has seen a coast-cliff or a river-ravine, has

[1] See *an'c*, p. 67.

had many a joint under his eyes. They are familiar to
the quarryman and miner, by whom their directions are
always well known, seeing that they determine the course
along which quarrying and many mining operations proceed. When the geologist is engaged in hilly or mountainous ground, among crags and rock-pinnacles, or on
exposed coast-cliffs, he should not fail to note with some
care the trend of the different joints. He will soon

Fig. 59.—Cliff cut into buttresses and recesses by means of the vertical joints of
the rocks.

find that they in each place run in two or more dominant directions. And a little further examination will
usually enable him to connect the forms of the cliffs
with the lines of joint. He will observe how one
set of joints runs parallel with the face of a cliff, and is
cut across by another series, and how the quadrangular
buttresses of rock, which may shoot up perhaps into
spiry pinnacles at the top, have their shape first given to
them by the intersecting lines of joint (Fig. 59).

With regard to the superficial deposits of a district,

the first aim of the geologist is to gather all available facts, not only from the sections exposed in natural openings, as well as in quarries and other artificial exposures, but, where needful, from the records of well-sinkings, borings, foundation-diggings, and all other kinds of excavations. The naming of the deposits, so far as their lithological characters go, will usually be an easy task ; but it may be more difficult to determine their relative order of appearance and the circumstances under which each was formed. A few examples of the kind of examination which may be made will here suffice.

Peat-mosses.—These accumulations of marshy vegetation play an important part in the surface geology of many

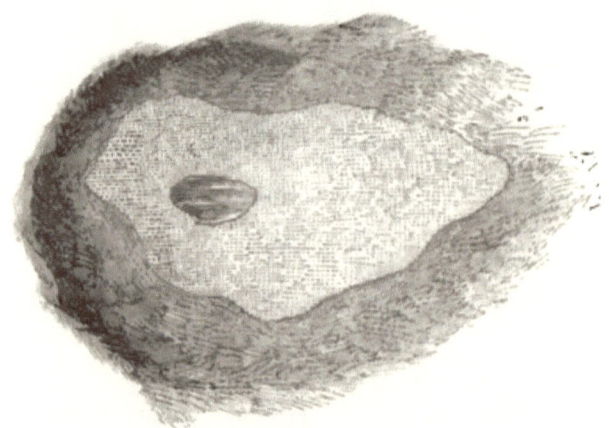

Fig. 60.—Plan of a peat-moss which has filled up a former shallow-lake, except one small patch of water.

tracts of Western Europe. In endeavouring to ascertain the history of a peat-moss we have first to consider the form of the surrounding ground, and to judge whether any lake could have probably existed on its site. In some cases, indeed, we may still detect a portion of the original lake surrounded and continually lessened by the advancing peat (Fig. 60). It is easy to see that at a comparatively recent period the aspect of these tracts of country must have been very different from what it is

FIG. 61.—Section of a peat-moss made in the excavation of peat for fuel.

to-day. Ireland, for example, must have been an island of shallow lakes instead of peat-bogs. Underneath the peat a layer of fresh-water marl may frequently be found full of such typically lacustrine shells as *Lymnea*, *Paludina*, *Planorbis*, and *Cyclas*. These underlying layers should always be diligently searched for bones of mammalia. The wild oxen and deer of the time of the

lakes and early morasses have often left their remains at
the bottom of the mosses.   Human relics ought also to
be looked for.   Canoes and stone implements are often
taken out of peat deposits.   Stockaded islets or cran-
noges may likewise now and then be found.   It is always
desirable to enlist the co-operation of the workpeople at
such places, as they are far more likely than an occasional
visitor to come upon objects of interest.

Brick-earth.—Where a thick deposit of loam or earth
covers the surface, especially on the slopes of broad river-
valleys, attention should be directed to its composition
and contents.   If it contains occasional land-shells, is

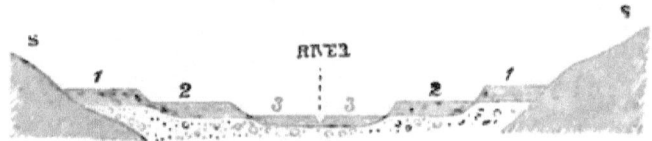

Fig. 62.—River terraces.

not very well stratified, shows no lines of gravel, nor any
water-worn stones, and has never yielded either a lacustrine, fluviatile, or marine shell, it may be presumed to
be a subærial formation due to the long-continued action
of rain or wind, gently moving the soil down to the lower
grounds.   In the lower parts of the valley of the river
Thames thick accumulations of this kind occur, and
their antiquity is indicated by the peculiar assemblage
of extinct mammalia, including forms of elephant, rhinoceros, and hippopotamus, which they contain.

River Terraces.—These conspicuous features of most
river valleys can be easily traced along either side.   The
observer ascertains the number of terraces (in the valleys
of British rivers there are commonly three), and their

general average height above each other and above the
present mean level of the river. He compares the character of their deposits, and seeks for any information
thence obtainable as to variation in the conditions of
the river. He keeps his eye constantly open to the possible discovery of organic remains in the terraces, more
especially in those of greater altitude, which being the
oldest ought to contain the earliest forms of life. Rudely-
chipped flint-instruments, or more deftly-fashioned celts
occurring in the undisturbed strata of a terrace, prove
that man inhabited the district when the river flowed
over these strata.

Surface Mounds.—In most districts the field-geologist
meets with mounds, as to the origin of which he at first
may be puzzled, if indeed he ever comes to any satisfactory conclusion regarding them. The first question
he will ask is, Are they of human construction ? Having
satisfied himself that they are not, he may try to find
some other origin for them by examining their composition, where any available section can be found, and the
nature of the surrounding ground. Mounds close to the
level of a river must always be regarded with a preliminary suspicion of being relics of a formation elsewhere
removed by the erosive action of the stream. Mounds
of sand and gravel scattered across a district may either
be due to the irregular denudation of a once continuous,
though perhaps unequal, covering of these loose materials,
or to the shapes assumed at the time of deposition. In
the former case we should expect to find that sections
cut into the mounds would show the present slopes
to have been cut across the bedding of any strata
which may occur. In the latter case we should

probably meet with instances of a conformity between the external slopes of the mounds and the inclination of the layers of sand or gravel inside ; and this conclusion as to the mounds being the original shape assumed by the loose materials at the time of their deposit would be amply confirmed if we saw little basins filled with water or with peat, lying between the mounds, for it is evident that had the slopes been due to atmospheric denudation these hollows must necessarily have been filled up, or rather could not have been formed. Mounds of this kind, deriving their peculiar forms from the circumstances of their formation, are abundant in the north of Britain and in Scandinavia. Some of them lie on open moors or hill-sides, and on watersheds. These are known as *eskers*, *kames*, or *ösar*. A second kind occurs in valleys among the hills, with the forms of rude crescent-shaped ridges curving from side to side of their valleys, sometimes in-closing small lakes : these are unmistakably the mo-raine-heaps of local glaciers. A third kind consists of a stiff, stony, boulder-clay or earth. The mounds of this type are arranged in one general line across wide tracts of low ground in Ireland and Scotland, where they are known as *drums*. They belong to the older glacial formations of the country.

Boulders and Travelled Stones.—In most countries where hard rocks of any kind protrude above the soil, scattered blocks of stone may be observed. When these are of large size, and have no visible rock near them, they are commonly assumed to be erratic masses which have been carried by ice to their present positions. Before accepting this interpretation, however, the observer should endeavour to ascertain whether they are really of a material foreign to the district. In many cases he will find that they are not; that on the contrary, their parent rocks, or at least rocks having precisely the same lithological characters, lie near at hand. Thus, the well-known Druid or Sarsen stones so abundantly strewn over the plains of Wiltshire, were formerly supposed to have been carried from some extraneous source, but are now recognised as fragments from a continuous stratum which once covered that part of the country. It is surprising over what a slight inclination large blocks may slowly move in the course of years, as the soil underneath is mixed by worms and roots, and gradually shifted towards lower levels. Sometimes escarpments which once supplied a crop of blocks to the slopes below, get gradually buried under their own *débris*, and are in the end earthed and grassed over, so that those blocks which may still remain exposed, and have survived the crags that supplied them, might be taken for far-transported erratics. It is essential, therefore, when the observer wishes to determine beyond question whether a particular boulder is due merely to the disintegration of a rock *in situ* or to transport from some distance, first of all to make sure that there is no parent rock in the immediate vicinity to which the rock can possibly be referred, either because its composition is different, or because its position shows that it could not have come by mere ordinary decay and removal. If he can prove that the block is foreign to the district, or that though rocks of the same character occur they could not have supplied the block in question except by the intervention of some unusual agent which moved it into its present position, he will establish that at all events the boulder is a transported one.

What may have been the agent of transport must be decided by the particular evidence in each case. In a river valley, blocks within reach of the present or former currents may have been moved downward by river floods. Waves can throw up blocks of considerable size, and even quarry them out of their solid beds in the parent rock at heights of seventy feet or more above high water. To the freezing of the sea around shore-blocks and the subsequent breaking up of the ice, the transport of considerable masses of rock along shore has been due. Icebergs have been observed at sea with blocks of stone and heaps of rock-rubbish lying upon them. Glaciers transport enormous quantities of loose blocks of rock and earth from the upper valleys. Undoubtedly ice has been the great agent in the distribution of erratic blocks; but whether in the form of floating-ice, of glaciers, or of a great general sheet of land-ice, must be decided in each district, not only from the evidence of the blocks themselves, but from the other data obtainable as to the glaciation of the country.

Glaciation.—Only a very few words are possible here on this wide and fascinating subject, regarding which of course the reader has ample means of information from the voluminous literature already devoted to it. Certainly among the many superficial characters of interest found in the northern parts of the northern hemisphere, as well as in mountain-tracts in other regions of the globe, few offer such temptations to their study as the smoothed and striated surfaces left upon rocks by the passage of sheets of ice across them. They occur in such unlooked-for places, and among surroundings now suggestive of almost any other physical condition than that of an Arctic ice-

sheet. When the field-geologist has once seen this kind
of surface, he is not likely to confound it with any other.
The only one for which it sometimes might be mistaken
is that termed *slickensides*, where the two walls or faces of
a joint or fault have slid upon one another so that each
side is rubbed smooth, polished, and grooved. But a
little practice and the study of good examples will give
the observer such confidence in discriminating between
them as he cannot acquire in any other way. The glacial

FIG. 63.—Ice-worn hummocks of rock, the arrow pointing in the direction of the
ice-movement.

striation is a merely superficial marking. The ruts are
often paler than the rest of the rock, as scratches on a
fresh rock-surface are, and though marked in each case
by one prevalent direction, are found often to cross each
other obliquely. There is generally great variety in the
size and depth of the striæ; some being such fine lines
as might have been graven by the point of a quartz-
crystal, others closely adjacent being blunt and coarse
as if produced by the edge of an angular block of stone.
Moreover the striated surfaces are undulating and dimpled,

the striæ descending into and rising out of these inequalities. Here and there, the groovings may be seen rising up a sloping boss of rock, but if the inclination of the rock becomes steep the markings diverge on either side of it. Now a slickensided surface presents in many respects a contrast to these features. It is almost always coated with some mineral glaze or incrustation, such as hæmatite, calcite, chlorite, or quartz, and this incrustation has taken a cast of the striæ on the rock, so as to look as if itself striated. In innumerable instances the slickenside is not confined to one surface, but may be detected in successive planes inside the rock, showing it to be an internal condition of the mass due to the shifting and grinding together of its parts, and not to a mere superficial agent like moving ice. The striæ of slickensides are close-set, parallel, and tolerably equal in breadth and depth, and they lie on flat surfaces which do not undulate in the manner so characteristic of glaciated rocks.

It is important to take with the compass the direction of the glacial groovings and striæ on the rocks. If possible the observer should at the same time determine from which quarter the ice has moved. This may often be done by observing in what direction little prominences and the edges of angular projections are rounded off, and to which side the still rough and unstriated portions look. The ice must evidently have moved from the quarter to which the smoothed faces are presented, and towards the quarter to which the rough parts are turned. This is shown in Fig. 63, where the arrow indicates the trend of the ice-movement. The way in which an observation of this kind may be indicated on the map is shown in the index of signs in Fig. 4. By a sufficient number of such

observations in a district, the path of the ice across it
may be very clearly expressed.

There is another useful method of supplementing this
evidence from rock-striations as to movements of the ice ;
but it cannot usually be put into practice until after the
observer has made some considerable acquaintance with
the geology of the whole region. In countries which
have been under ice, and where the rocks retain the
characteristic ice-markings, the surface commonly presents
abundant accumulations of boulder-clay, gravel, and

FIG. 64.—Striated stone from the boulder-clay.

other deposits belonging to different conditions of the
long glacial period. A search through the stones and
boulders of those deposits will in most cases disclose the
fact that these fragmentary materials have been moved a
greater or less distance from their parent rocks. In the
clays the stones are often as well striated as the solid
rock below (Fig. 64). Let us pick out at random two or
three hundred stones from any section of boulder-clay or
moraine-stuff, and note down the proportions in which
each variety of rock occurs among them. We shall find
perhaps that 50 or 60 per cent. may have been derived

N

from rocks in the immediate vicinity, that 20 or 30 per cent. have perhaps come a good many miles, while the remainder (usually small in size) may possibly be traced to some of the most distant rocks in the drainage-basin of the region. We learn from such an analysis the general direction of the ice-stream and see that it agrees with the evidence furnished by the striæ on the rocks.

PART II.

INDOOR·WORK.

CHAPTER XV.

NATURE OF INDOOR-WORK. GEOLOGICAL SECTIONS.

WHEN a geologist returns to his quarters after a long day in the field, if he means to make further use of the information which he has collected in the course of his walk, he ought on no account to allow himself, no matter how seductive may be the attractions of his comfortable quarters, to dismiss from his mind the labours of the day until he has looked over his notes, and filled in, while still fresh in his memory, all details which he did not find time to jot down on the ground. This task sometimes demands not a little self-denial on the part of one who feels that he has worked well and earned his *siesta* with a pleasant book or the latest newspaper. But it must be done, and done then. Put off till next day, the duty is more irksome, and the details are already beginning to be elbowed out of memory by the host of new ones which have been observed.

It is particularly useful to enter in the note-book sections of the ground just examined, giving what may be at the time the observer's interpretation of the structure of the rocks.   Even though these are thrown aside in the end, or superseded by others based on wider experience, they serve their purpose by fixing in the mind what has been seen, and directing attention to the points on which the evidence is defective.   A good working hypothesis, so useful in all kinds of scientific work, when employed as a help and not as a master, is specially serviceable in field-geology.   One such hypothesis after another may have to be abandoned, but each performs its work in leading the observer nearer to the true solution of his problem. And it is as embodying his working hypothesis of the day that these rough tentative sections in the note-book, made while all the first impressions are still fresh and clear, derive their chief value.

If the geologist is gifted with any power of sketching he will take care that his pencil drawings or outlines— all perhaps that his time and work will allow in the field —are secured before getting rubbed, as they are sure to do if carried without precaution in his everyday note-book.   They may of course be fixed in the ordinary way with weak gum-water, isinglass, white of egg, or skimmed milk.   But I have found it preferable to wash them with sepia or indian-ink.   By this means the pencil-lines are fixed, while at the same time with the brush and two or three tints of colour, the sky and relative tones of the landscape may be given.   Of course if water-colour can be rapidly used in the field this is still better ; but in my own experience the temptation to make a sketch instead of a geological diagram is so great that the

amount of field-work suffers diminution. Hence I would
advise that the field-work be done first, and that the
observer, having thus been over the ground and chosen
his points of view, should return with his sketch-book
and colour-box, and use them with no inward conscious-
ness that he ought to be up and wielding his hammer.
An occasional thoroughly wet day, when work out of doors
is impossible, affords an excellent opportunity for fixing
the drawings, determining rocks, drawing sections, writing
up notes, and indeed for all other kinds of indoor-
employment.

In a former chapter I spoke of certain portions of his
labours which the field-geologist could only accomplish
within doors.   I propose now to describe three kinds of
indoor-work.   1, Section-drawing; 2, Blowpipe analysis;
and 3, the examination of rocks by the microscope.

SECTION DRAWING.

The construction of geological sections is placed here
among the indoor employments of the field-geologist,
although if they are to be as full and perfect as possible,
their outlines must be traced on the ground.   A section
on a true scale, vertical and horizontal, may be prepared
by measurement on the ground in the ordinary way with
chain and theodolite.   But this is an operation of ordinary
land-surveying which need not be described here.   Or if
the country has been accurately contoured, a section may
be drawn by using the contour-lines.

The more clearly a geological map represents the
structure of a country, the less need is there for any
additional explanation, so that a perfect map, large
in scale and detailed in execution, should be nearly

independent of sections or other assistance, except for data, which cannot be expressed upon a map. But such a map can comparatively seldom be made, and clearly constructed sections always save much time and labour, as they enable the structure of a region to be seen and comprehended almost at a glance. We must usually be content with a map on a small scale, an imperfect topography, and other defects which compel us to supplement the map with lines of section so drawn as to convey to the eyes of others exactly what we have ourselves seen or believe to be the geological structure of the district or country in question.

A section may either be horizontal or vertical, that is, it may show either what would be seen if a deep trench could be cut across hill and valley, so as to expose the relations of the rocks to each other, or else the arrangement and thicknesses of the rocks if we could pile them up into a tall column one above another in their proper order of succession. On a small scale, Fig. 49 may be taken as an example of a vertical section. This kind of section is chiefly of use in detailed work, as, for instance, among coal-fields, where the various strata of one pit or part of a district are to be compared with those of another, or in localities like the coast-sections of the Tertiary rocks of the Isle of Wight, where every stratum is exposed to view. Evidently a section of this kind requires good exposures of rock and careful measurement.

The horizontal section, on the other hand, must often be constructed where exposures of rock are few, where minute measurements are impossible, and where the highest skill of the field-geologist is taxed to unravel the

meaning of the facts he notes upon the surface, and
to show their bearing upon the relations of the rocks
below ground. The first point I would remark in the
drawing of a horizontal section is, that where possible,
the section should always be on a true scale, that is, the
height and length should be on the same scale. Of
course this is often impossible, for the ground may be
low, and to show its true form in a section might require
an extravagant and unnecessary length of paper. Still
the geologist who would preserve, as he should, the
relations between the external form of the ground and
the structure of the rocks below it, will always endeavour
to exaggerate the height of his sections as little as
possible. I believe that nothing has tended so much to
perpetuate erroneous notions regarding the physiography
of the land as such distorted sections, sometimes almost
grotesque in their exaggeration of natural forms.

As an example of the disregard which some able
observers have had for truth of outline in their sections,
there are inserted on the following page two sections of the
same hill. On one of these (A), an eminent mineralogist,
seems to have been content to represent in a kind of
diagrammatic way the order of the formations, heedless
of the utterly unnatural shape of his hill. The other
section (B) shows the true outline of the ground, on the
scale of six inches to a mile, vertical and horizontal, with
the relative position of the rocks correctly inserted.

A further and familiar illustration of the effects of this
neglect of the true proportions of the ground is offered
to us by the case of the "London Basin." I presume
most readers, when they meet with that phrase, think of
a deep bowl-shaped hollow filled with clay and surrounded

by a rim of chalk hills, and they probably recall one of the sections in popular manuals and text-books by which this impression was originally given to them. If, however, we construct a section across the London basin on a true scale, or examine that which has been constructed and published by the Geological Survey on the scale of

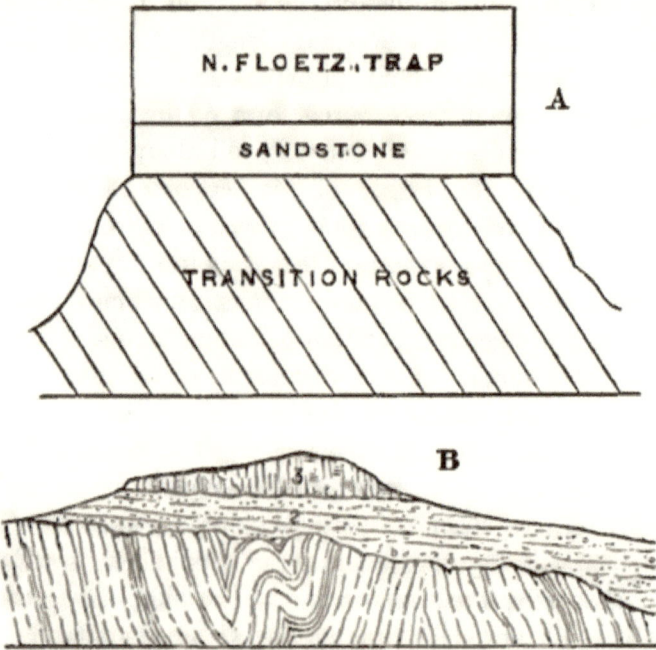

FIG. 65.—Illustrations of geological section drawing.

six inches to a mile, we learn that so flat is the basin, so small the thickness of clay (500 feet) in proportion to the breadth of country over which it is spread (24 miles), that we need to look with some little care to be assured that there is really any basin at all.

The next point to be attended to in the construction of a horizontal section is the choice of the line of ground across which it is to be drawn. It may be designed either to show the general structure of the country or the arrangement of the rocks in some particular part of it. In any case, while taking it over those portions of the ground where the structure is best seen, we should always bear in mind that it must pass as nearly as possible at a right angle to the strike of inclined strata. Obviously, a section coincident with the strike would make highly-inclined beds look horizontal.

When the time arrives for a section to be drawn, the first thing is to insert the outline of the ground. The actually observed geological data, such as dips, faults, and other facts, are then placed upon that outline. If necessary, search is made on either side of the line of section for additional materials to fill in the blanks in the section. The lines found at the surface are then prolonged downward, and the section is filled in. To make these stages more clearly understood, let us suppose that we are required to draw a section on a true scale (say of six inches to a mile) across a piece of ground. We fix on some datum-line, the sea-level, for instance, on which to erect our verticals for the heights. Having obtained the correct measurements of the surface from our own levellings, or those of other surveyors (in this country the contoured maps of the Ordnance Survey are invaluable for this purpose) we proceed to mark off from our datum-line a series of points, the height of each of which is known. How this is done is shown in Fig. 66, A. A line is then drawn, connecting all the points together, which gives, it will be observed, the general

contour of the ground. To ensure greater fidelity of
detail it may be well to walk again over the ground with
the plotted section in hand, so as to be able to fill in
any little inequalities of surface, and at the same time
to look once more for evidence as to the nature and
structure of the rocks below. The drawing in Fig. 66 B

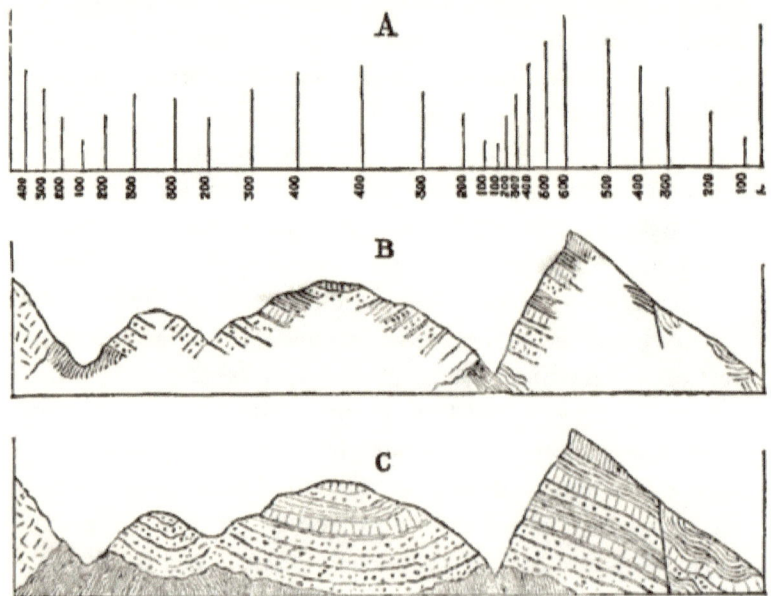

FIG. 66.—Stages in the construction of a geological section.

may be taken to represent the outline as so modified by
a visit to the ground. On this same drawing all the
geological data are inserted which are supposed to be
actually seen, either on the line traversed by the section
or in the immediate vicinity of it. But a more extended
examination of the district would no doubt supply many

data not obtainable on the precise course of section, and permit the lines to be prolonged downward, and the whole section to be filled in somewhat in the manner shown in C. The section in Fig. 27, shows the structure of the country represented in the map, and illustrates the application of many of the terms which I have made use of in these pages.

CHAPTER XVI.

CHEMICAL TESTS IN THE IDENTIFICATION OF MINERALS AND ROCKS.

IT often happens, especially in the early years of his experience, that the geologist meets with rocks which none of the tests available in the field enable him satisfactorily to recognise. In such cases, as already remarked, he detaches one or more fresh chips of each puzzling variety, and carries them home for determination by more precise processes. He may, in the first place, apply some simple chemical tests. Detailed chemical analysis cannot of course be attempted in the ordinary conditions of field-work, but much may be learnt by a few easily performed experiments.

1 *Treatment with Acid.*—In the list of a geologist's accoutrements for the field, a small acid-bottle was included (*ante* p. 27). A drop of weak hydrochloric acid will at once tell by a brisk effervescence if a rock is a limestone or is markedly calcareous. By the same means we may often trace the decomposition of such rocks as dolerite to a considerable distance inward from the surface ; the original lime-bearing silicate of the rock having been decomposed by the infiltrating rain-

water, and partially converted into carbonate of lime.
This carbonate is far more sensitive to the acid test than
the other carbonates usually to be met with among
rocks. A drop of weak cold acid suffices to produce
abundant effervescence even from a crystalline face. But
the effervescence becomes much more marked if we apply
the acid to the powder of the stone. For this purpose
a scratch may be made and then touched with acid. By
this means a copious discharge of carbonic acid may
be obtained from some rocks where otherwise it might
appear so feebly as perhaps even to escape observation.
Some carbonates, dolomite for example, are hardly
affected by acid until powdered. In other cases the
acid requires to be heated, or must be used very strong,
as with siderite.

It is a convenient method of roughly estimating the
purity of a limestone to place a fragment of the rock in
weak hydrochloric acid. If there is much impurity,
(clay, sand, oxide of iron, &c.), this will remain behind
as an insoluble residue, and may then be further tested
chemically or examined with the microscope. Of course
the acid may attack some of the impurities, so that it
cannot be concluded that the residue absolutely represents everything present in the rock except the carbonate of lime, but the proportion of non-calcareous
matter so dissolved by the acid will usually be extremely
small.

If the student possesses chemical knowledge, he
may proceed to test the acid solution he obtains from
a pulverized rock and may detect the bases; but as
a rule such analysis is only of secondary importance for
geological purposes.

Some acquaintance with chemical reactions, indeed, will be found of great service in the identification of rocks and of their constituent minerals. It is commonly the case that minerals about which the observer may be doubtful are precisely those which, from their small size, are most difficult of separation from the rest of the rock preparatory to analytical processes. The mineral apatite, for example, occurs in minute hexagonal prisms which on cross-fracture might be mistaken for nepheline, or even sometimes for quartz. If, however, a drop of solution of molybdate of ammonia be placed upon the crystal, a yellow precipitate will appear if it be apatite. Nepheline, which is another hexagonal mineral likewise abundant in some rocks gives no yellow precipitate with the ammonia solution, while if a drop of hydrochloric acid be put over it, crystals of chloride of sodium or common salt will be obtained. These reactions can be observed even with minute crystals, by placing them under the microscope and using an exceedingly attenuated pipette for dropping the liquid on the rock.

2. *Blow-pipe Tests.*—The chief chemical tests available for the field-geologist are those which he can perform with the blow-pipe. These he will find to be simple, easily applied, and requiring only patience and practice to give him great assistance in his determination of minerals. If unacquainted with blow pipe analysis he must refer to one or other of the numerous text-books on the subject, some of which are mentioned below.[1]

---

[1] The great work on the blow-pipe is Plattner's, of which an English translation has been published. Elderhorst's *Manual of*

The apparatus required for ordinary blow-pipe work is exceedingly simple. For his early practice the student will find the following sufficient : —

1. Blow pipe.
2. Thick-wicked candle, or a tin box filled with the material of Child's night-lights, and furnished with a piece of Freyberg wick in a metallic support.
3. Platinum-tipped forceps.
4. A few pieces of platinum wire in lengths of three or four inches.
5. A few pieces of platinum foil.
6. Some pieces of charcoal.
7. A number of closed and open tubes of hard glass.
8. Three small stoppered bottles containing carbonate of soda, borax, and microcosmic salt.
9. Magnet.

To this list he can add as he finds occasion. The whole may easily be packed into a box which will go into the corner of a portmanteau.

The annexed Scheme shows the procedure which the observer may follow in the blow-pipe determination of a mineral. He will find it advantageous to write down under each head the behaviour of the substance before he proceeds to the next operation.

Qualitative Blow-pipe Analysis and Determinative Mineralogy, by H. B. Nason and C. F. Chandler (Philadelphia: N. S. Porter and Coates), is a smaller but useful volume; while still less pretending is Scheerer's *Introduction to the Use of the Mouth Blow-pipe*, of which a third edition by H. F. Blanford was published in 1875 by F. Norgate. An admirable work of reference will be found in Professor Brush's *Manual of Determinative Mineralogy* (New York: J. Wiley and Son).

Locality, &c., of specimen.	I. Behaviour in closed tube.	II. In open tube.	III. On charcoal.		IV. On platinum forceps or wire (or on foil with soda).			Other reactions. Remarks.
			(a) Alone.	(b) With soda.	(a) Alone.	(b) With borax.	(c) With microcosmic salt.	

3. *Magnetic Analysis.*—Many dark crystalline rocks
contain much magnetite or other magnetic mixtures of
iron oxides. Some idea of the relative proportions of these
ingredients may be formed by reducing a specimen of
the rock to the finest powder in an agate mortar, and
then weighing out so many grains of the powder. Care
must be taken not to allow any iron instrument to touch
the rock, which indeed should be collected in the field by
breaking up a large piece with another stone and avoiding
the use of a hammer, or if a hammer has been used, the
specimen should be carefully washed and rubbed with a
brush before being reduced to powder. The magnet, pro-
tected by fine tissue-paper, may then be inserted into the
powder, and the magnetic particles which adhere to it
should be dropped into a separate dish, which is easily
done by pulling the magnet slightly away from the paper,
when the iron particles at once fall off. The process
should be repeated until no more magnetic grains adhere
to the magnet. An additional proportion of iron grains
may, however, be obtained by grinding the powder in the
mortar with water, allowing it thereafter to dry thoroughly,
and then when it has once more been bruised with the
mortar, placing the paper-protected magnet upon it.
Minute black specks will be observed adhering to the
paper. The magnetic grains in the separate dish should
be examined with a lens to see that no considerable
quantity of the other minerals of the rock may be ad-
herent to them, in which case they may be gently pounded
with water in the mortar, dried, and picked out afresh with
the magnet. The magnetic residue obtained represents
nearly the proportion of magnetic iron in the rock; but
is almost always under the truth, because some of the

O

magnetic iron is in microscopic particles, inclosed within other constituents of the rock. This rough method of analysis may be satisfactorily applied to basalt, dolerite, and similar rocks.

Important Minerals in Rocks.—To assist the learner in his field-work the following list is given. It contains the more important minerals which occur as essential or accidental constituents of rocks, and indicates briefly the conditions under which each may be expected to be found.

List of the more Important Minerals which enter into the Composition of Rock-masses.

		I. Essential Constituent. II. Accessory Ingredient.
NATIVE ELEMENTS.	Graphite . . .	II. Scales and layers in gneiss, schists, slates ; also as a result of the alteration of coal by intrusive igneous rocks.
	Sulphur . . .	II. Chiefly at volcanic orifices and as a product of decomposition among Tertiary strata.
SULPHIDES.	Pyrite	II. Abundantly diffused in rocks of all ages in detached crystals and in veins.
	Marcasite . .	II. Especially among sedimentary rocks, often taking the place of organic remains : very liable to decomposition.
	Chalcopyrite .	II. Veins chiefly.
	Galena . . .	II. Scattered grains, but chiefly in veins.
	Blende . . .	II. Usually with galena in veins.

FLUORIDE.	{	Fluor spar . .	II. Veinstone in stratified and unstratified rocks: occasionally in cavities of crystalline rocks.
CHLORIDE.	{	Rock-salt . .	I. In beds especially associated with red strata: sometimes II. as scattered cubes in red sandstones, clays, and other strata, but then generally replaced by clay; &c.
OXIDES. — Anhydrous.	{	Quartz . . .	I. Abundant in many crystalline rocks, *e.g.* granite, quartz-porphyry, liparite; and in fragmental rocks, as sandstone, greywacke, &c. II. Frequent in veins and cavities of rocks of all ages as an infiltration product.
		,, Calcedony	II. Filling or lining cavities especally of old volcanic rocks; introduced by infiltration.
		Hæmatite . .	I. In some crystalline rocks: in beds among foliated rocks and as a colouring-matter in fragmental rocks. II. Abundant in veins and cavities of rocks as an infiltration product.
		Magnetite . .	I. In many foliated rocks, *e.g.* chlorite slate; abundantly in minute crystals in many igneous rocks, as dolerite, basalt, &c.
		Ilmenite . . .	I. In many foliated rocks; also abundant in some volcanic rocks, as dolerite, gabbro, &c.
OXIDES. — Hydrous.	{	Limonite . .	II. Common as an alteration-product of previously-formed hæmatite in veins and cavities of rocks.
		Wad . . . . Psilomelane . .	II. As a dark earthy substance in cavities and veins of rocks, and as dendritic markings in the minute fissures of such close-grained rocks as felsite-porphyry and lithographic limestone.

	I. Essential Constituent. II. Accessory Ingredient.
Orthoclase or Monoclinic Felspar. Orthoclase and Varieties	I. Abundant among both ancient and modern crystalline rocks, as granite, gneiss, quartz-porphyry, liparite, trachyte, obsidian, &c.
Plagioclase, or Triclinic Felspars. Oligoclase / Albite	I. Abundant as the triclinic felspars of older crystalline rocks, as in granite, syenite, &c.
Anorthite / Labradorite	I. Abundant, more especially among volcanic rocks of all ages from palæozoic up to recent; found also among ancient foliated rocks, as the gneiss of Labrador and in some granites.
Leucite	I. An essentially volcanic mineral, only found in lavas and tuffs of later geological periods.
Nepheline . . .	I. In some volcanic rocks in minute prisms; also massive in metamorphic rocks.
Hauyne	I. Only found in post-tertiary lavas.
Nosean	II. Like Haüyne, a volcanic mineral of late geological date, said to occur in almost all phonolites.
Muscovite . . . (Potass-mica)	I. Abundant in old crystalline rocks, both massive and foliated—granite, gneiss, mica-schist, greisen, &c.; also in sandstones of all ages.
Biotite . . . . (Magnesia-mica)	I. Abundant in many crystalline rocks. II. As an occasional alteration-product in many hornblendic and augitic rocks.
Chiastolite . . .	I. Abundantly diffused through some metamorphic slates, hence called chiastolite-slates.
Kyanite	I. In small granular forms in some crystalline rocks, e.g. kyanite-rock; also in beds and veins in gneiss.
Tourmaline . . .	I. In some granites, and in the veins associated with and proceeding from these granites.

ALUMINOUS SILICATES. Anhydrous.

	I. Essential Constituent. II. Accessory Ingredient.

ALUMINOUS SILICATES. Anhydrous.

Garnet . . . I. Abundant in many foliated rocks, as in mica-schist and some varieties of gneiss.

Epidote . . . I. In some foliated rocks, as gneiss and mica schist.
II. As an alteration-product in many rocks, as in diorite, diabase, altered sandstone, &c.

Cordierite . . I. In geodes and veins among older crys-
(Iolite) talline rocks, as granite, gneiss, and several schists; one variety, cordierite-gneiss, contains it abundantly.

ALUMINOUS SILICATES. Hydrous.

Zeolites . . . II. This interesting family of minerals is due to the alteration of anhydrous alu-minous silicates, chiefly felspars. The several species occur as secondary pro-ducts in veins and cavities of rocks, es-pecially of such as contain abundant felspar. The amygdaloidal cavities of basalts and other basic volcanic rocks furnish many varieties.

Ottrelite . . I. In some varieties of slate, as that of Ottrez, Luxembourg, whence the name ottrelite slate.

Kaolin . . . II. Decomposed felspar, apt to occur wher-ever a felspar-bearing rock is exposed to a moist climate.

MAGNESIAN SILICATES. Anhydrous.

Hornblende . I. Abundant as a constituent of many mas-sive crystalline rocks, *e.g.* syenite and diorite; of many foliated rocks, as horn-blende-schist, and varieties of gneiss.

Augite . . . I. The black variety abundant among vol-canic rocks—basalt, diabase, &c.; the paler kinds among granitic and foliated rocks and not uncommon among crystal-line limestones.

Diallage . . I. One of the constituents of gabbro; also found in serpentine and hypersthene rock.

		I. Essential Constituent. II. Accessory Ingredient.
MAGNESIAN SILICATES. — Anhydrous.	Enstatite . .	I. One of the constituents of the rock called Lherzolite; occurs also in some serpentines and in some meteorites.
	Bronzite . .	I. In some serpentines and basalts; also in some meteorites.
	Uralite . . .	II. A mineral having the crystalline form of augite but the internal fine fibrous character of hornblende, with sometimes a central core of still unaltered augite. In some old porphyritic rocks—Urals, Norway, Alps, Scotland.
	Smaragdite .	I. A constituent of the rock called eclogite and some forms of gabbro.
Hydrous.	Talc	I. Abundant among foliated rocks, some of which (e.g., talc-schist) consist largely of it. II. As an alteration-product among crystalline rocks.
	Chlorite . . .	I. Constituting almost the whole of the rock termed chlorite-slate, and found among other foliated and crystalline rocks. II. Frequent as an alteration-product in rocks containing hornblende, augite, olivine, or other anhydrous magnesian silicate.
	Serpentine . .	I. Constitutes entire rock-masses, but these appear in all cases to have been originally anhydrous, often olivine-rocks. II. Frequent as an alteration-product, particularly in rocks containing olivine.
	Delessite . — Saponite . — (Celadonite)	II. Alteration-products in crystalline rocks, especially volcanic masses rich in magnesian silicates; occur in kernels filling cavities, as incrustations, round nodules, or in irregular veinings and blotches.
	Glauconite . . (Silicate of Iron and Potass.)	II. Abundantly diffused through some sandstones, and found also as an alteration-product among many old augitic and hornblendic volcanic rocks, lining cavities or running in threads through the altered mass.

		I. Essential Constituent. II. Accessory Ingredient.
CARBONATES.	Calcite	I. Common as limestone or the calcareous constituent of stratified rocks. II. Very abundant as an alteration-product, filling cavities or running in veins and threads through rocks.
	Aragonite . . .	II. Under similar circumstances as calcite, but less abundant.
	Dolomite. . . .	I. Occurs in beds and layers with limestone, red marl, sandstone, &c. II. In veins and cavities and along the edges of intrusive igneous rocks.
	Siderite	I. In beds and nodules associated with shale, coal, &c. II. Occasionally in veins and cavities of rocks.
SULPHATES. Anhydrous.	Barytes . . .	II. Common as a veinstone; also found in cavities of amygdaloidal rocks.
	Celestine . .	II. In cavities and veins in limestone, sandstone, and in some old volcanic rocks.
	Anhydrite . .	I. In beds, associated with limestone, red sandstone, or rock-salt.
Hydrous.	Gypsum . .	I. In beds with red strata, rock-salt, &c. II. In veins and strings through different rocks.
	Alums . . .	II. Aluminous rocks, containing iron sulphides, exposed to weathering are apt to decompose, and various alum-salts appear as an efflorescence.
PHOSPHATES.	Apatite	I. Abundant in some metamorphic regions, both in layers and in veins; an essential constituent of many crystalline rocks, as varieties of granite, diorite, diabase, gabbro, and dolerite. II. Common as a veinstone in some metalliferous districts.
	Vivianite. . . .	II. In veins associated with metallic ores; also as a blue earth in bogs and other places where animal remains have decayed, and as a peach-bloom on some ichthyolites.

		I. Essential Constituent. II. Accessory Ingredient.
TITANATE.	Sphene	I. Abundant in some granites, syenites, gneisses, schists, and metamorphic lime-stones.
HYDRO-CARBONS.	Asphalt	II. Occasionally disseminated in grains or filling veins and cavities of sandstone or other rocks.
	Naphtha	II. Occasionally in cavities of rocks, or coming to surface either alone or with spring water.
	Anthracite . . .	I. In beds, like ordinary coal. II. In cavities of rocks, particularly in association with intrusive igneous masses; also diffused in minute grains, giving a black, coally aspect to some rocks.

CHAPTER XVII.

FREQUENT reference has been made in the foregoing pages to the advantage of studying minerals and rocks under the microscope. By this means we are enabled to trace the minuter structures of the earth's crust, and to follow many of the stages in the formation of its rocks. We can tell which mineral of a rock crystallized first, and indeed can follow every phase of crystallization, in such a way as to explain many otherwise unknown parts of the history of the rocks. Moreover by this method we can trace the subsequent changes which rocks have suffered, in the chemical alteration of their minerals by percolating water, with the resulting secondary products. While a chemical analysis informs us of the ultimate chemical constitution of a rock, a microscopic analysis brings before us its mineralogical composition, showing in what forms the chemical elements have been combined, and how diverse two rocks may be in structure and texture, though in chemical composition nearly alike.

The field-geologist, however, besides these inquiries, often needs some ready means of determining the nature and petrographical grade of rocks which he cannot

satisfactorily name by any of the usual methods available
to him.   By far the most valuable aid in this respect is
supplied to him in the examination of thin slices with
the microscope.   He ought to be able to prepare his
own slices, though when he can have this satisfactorily
done for him he may save time for other work.

THE PREPARATION OF THIN SLICES.

To prepare slices of rocks and minerals for the microscope it is not necessary to procure a costly and unwieldy
set of apparatus, nor to go through a lengthened course
of training.   The operation is facilitated, indeed, by the
possession of a machine for cutting thin slices, and for
reducing and polishing them when mounted on glass.
A machine well adapted for both purposes was devised
some years ago by Mr. J. B. Jordan, and may be had of
Messrs. Cotton and Johnson, Grafton Street, Soho,
London, for £10 10s.   Another slicing and polishing
machine invented by Mr. F. G. Cuttell, 52, New
Compton Street, Soho, London, costs £6 10s.   But
these machines are rather unwieldy to be carried about
the country by a field-geologist.   Fuess of Berlin supplies
two small and convenient hand-instruments, one for
slicing, the other for grinding and polishing.   The slicing
machine is not quite so satisfactory for hard rocks
as one of the larger more solid forms of apparatus
worked by a treadle.   But the grinding-machine is exceedingly useful, and might be added to a geologist's
outfit without material inconvenience.   If a lapidary is
within reach, much of the more irksome part of the work

may be saved by getting him to cut off thin slices. The thickness of each slice must depend greatly upon the nature of the rock, the rule being to make the slice as thin as the rock will allow, so as to save labour in grinding down afterwards.

Excellent rock-sections, however, may be prepared without any machine, provided the operator possesses ordinary neatness of hand and patience. He must procure as thin chips as possible of the rocks he proposes to slice. These he can usually obtain in the field where he is hammering. He should select as fresh a portion of the rock as may be accessible, and by a dexterous use of the hammer break off from a sharp edge a number of thin splinters or chips, out of which he can choose one or more for making into rock-slices. These chips may be about an inch square. It is well to take several of them, as the first specimen may chance to be spoiled in the preparation. The geologist ought also always to carry off a piece of the same block from which his chip is taken, that he may have a specimen of the rock for future reference and comparison. Every such hand-specimen, as well as the chips belonging to it, ought to be wrapped up in paper on the spot where it is obtained, and inside the wrapper should be placed a label or piece of paper with the locality and any notes that may be thought necessary. It can hardly be too frequently reiterated that all such field-notes ought as far as possible to be written down on the ground where the actual facts are before us for examination.

Having obtained his thin slices, either by having them slit with a machine or by detaching with a hammer as thin splinters as possible, the operator may proceed to the preparation of them for the microscope. For this purpose the following simple apparatus is all that is absolutely needful, though if a grinding-machine be added it will save time and labour.

List of Apparatus Required in the Preparation of Thin Slices of Rocks and Minerals for Microscopical Examination.

1. A cast-iron plate, ¼ inch thick and 9 inches square.
2. Two pieces of plate-glass, 9 inches square.
3. A Water-of-Ayr stone, 6 inches long by 2½ inches broad.
4. Coarse emery (1 lb. or so at a time).
5. Fine or flour emery (ditto).
6. Putty powder (1 oz.).
7. Canada balsam. (There is an excellent kind prepared by Rimmington, Bradford, especially for microscopic preparations, and sold in shilling bottles.)
8. A small forceps.
9. Some oblong pieces of common flat window-glass; 2×1 inches is a convenient size.
10. Glasses with ground edges for mounting the slices upon. They may be had at any chemical instrument-maker in different sizes, the commonest being 3×1 inches.
11. Thin covering-glasses, square or round. These are sold by the ounce; ¼ ounce will be sufficient to begin with.
12. A small bottle of spirits of wine.

The first process consists in rubbing down and polishing one side of the chip or slice. We place the chip upon the wheel of the grinding-machine or, failing that, upon the iron plate, with a little coarse emery and water. If the chip is so shaped that it can be conveniently pressed by the finger against the plate and kept there in regular horizontal movement, we may proceed at once to rub it

down. If, however, we find a difficulty, from its small size
or otherwise, in holding the chip, one side of it may be
fastened to the end of a bobbin or other convenient bit
of wood by means of a cement formed of three-parts of
rosin and one of bees-wax, which is easily softened by
heating.   A little practice will show that a slow, equable
motion with a certain steady pressure is most effectual in
producing the desired flatness of surface.   When all the
roughnesses have been removed, which can be told after
the chip has been dipped in water so as to remove the
mud and emery, we place the specimen upon the square
of plate-glass, and with flour-emery and water continue
to rub it down until all the scratches caused by the
coarse emery have been removed and a smooth polished
surface has been produced.   Care should be taken to
wash the chip entirely free of any grains of coarse emery
before beginning to the polishing on glass.   It is desirable also to reserve the glass for polishing only.   The
emery gets finer and finer the longer it is used, so that
by remaining on the plate it may be used many times in
succession.   Of course the glass itself is worn down, but
by using alternately every portion of its surface and on
both sides, one plate may be made to last a considerable
time.   If after drying and examining it carefully, we find
the surface of the chip to be polished and free from
scratches, we may advance to the next process.   But it
will often happen that the surface is still finely scratched.
In this case we may place the chip upon the Water-of-
Ayr stone and with a little water gently rub it to and fro.
It should be held quite flat.   The Water-of-Ayr stone
too should not be allowed to get worn into a hollow, but
should be kept quite flat, otherwise we shall lose part

of the chip.   Some soft rocks, however, will not take an unscratched surface even with the Water-of-Ayr stone. These may be finished with putty-powder, applied with a bit of woollen rag.

The desired flatness and polish having been secured, and all trace of scratches and dirt having been completely removed, we proceed to grind down the opposite side and reduce the chip to the requisite degree of thinness.   The first step at this stage is to cement the polished surface of the chip to one of the pieces of common glass.   A thin piece of iron (a common shovel does quite well) is heated over a fire, or is placed between two supports over a gas-flame.   On this plate must be laid the piece of glass to which the specimen is to be affixed, and the specimen itself.   A little Canada balsam is dropped on the centre of the glass and allowed to remain until it has acquired the necessary consistency.   To test this condition, the point of a knife should be inserted into the balsam, and on being removed should be rapidly cooled by being pressed against some cold surface.   If it soon becomes hard it has been sufficiently heated. Care, however, must be observed not to let it remain too long on the hot plate; for it will then become brittle and start from the glass at some future stage, or at least will break away from the edges of the chip and leave them exposed to the risk of being frayed off.   The heat should be kept as moderate as possible, for if it becomes too great it may injure some portions of the rock.   Chlorite, for example, is rendered quite opaque if the heat is so great as to drive off its water.

When the balsam is found to be ready, the chip, which has been warmed on the same plate, is lifted with the forceps and its polished side is laid gently down upon the balsam. It is well to let one end touch the balsam first, and then gradually to lower the other, as in this way the air is driven out. With the point of a knife the chip should be moved about a little, so as to expel any bubbles of air and promote a firm cohesion between the glass and the stone. The glass is now removed with the forceps from the plate and put upon the table, and a lead weight or other small heavy object is placed upon the chip, so as to keep it pressed down until the balsam has cooled and hardened. If the operation has been successful the slide ought to be ready for further treatment as soon as the balsam has become cold. If, however, the balsam is still soft, the glass must be again placed on the plate and gently heated, until on cooling the balsam resists the pressure of the finger-nail.

Having now produced a firm union of the chip and the glass, we proceed to rub down the remaining side of the stone with coarse emery on the iron plate as before. If the glass cannot be held in the hand or moved by the simple pressure of the fingers, which usually suffices, it may be fastened to the end of the bobbin with the rosin cement as before. When the chip has thus been reduced until it is tolerably thin, until, for example, light begins to appear through it when held between the eye and the window, we may, as before, wash it clear of the coarse emery and continue the reduction of it on the glass plate with fine emery. Crystalline rocks, such as granite, gneiss, diorite, dolerite, and modern lavas, can be reduced to the required thinness on the glass. Softer rocks may require gentle treatment with the Water-of-Ayr stone.

The last parts of the process are the most delicate of all. We desire to make the section as thin as possible, and for that purpose continue rubbing until after one final attempt we perhaps find to our dismay that great part of the slice has disappeared. The utmost caution must consequently be used. The slide should be kept as flat as possible, and looked at frequently, that the first indications of disruption may be detected. The thinness desirable or attainable depends in great measure upon the nature of the rock. Transparent minerals need not be so much reduced as more opaque ones. Some minerals, indeed, remain absolutely opaque to the last, like pyrite, magnetite, and ilmenite.

The slide is now ready for the microscope. It ought always to be examined with that instrument at this stage. We can thus see whether it is thin enough, and if any chemical tests are required they can readily be applied to the exposed surface of the slice. If the rock has proved to be very brittle, and we have only succeeded in procuring a thin slice after much labour and several failures, nothing further should be done with the preparation unless to cover it with glass, as will be immediately explained, which not only protects it, but adds to its transparency. But where the slice is not so fragile, and will bear removal from its original rough scratched piece of glass, it should be transferred to one of the glass-slides (No. 10). For this purpose the preparation is once more placed on the warm iron plate, and close alongside of it is put the glass-slide, which has been carefully cleaned, and on the middle of which a little Canada balsam has been dropped. The heat gradually loosens the cohesion of the slice, which is then very gently pushed along to the contiguous clean slip of glass. Considerable practice is needed in this part of the work, as the slice, being so thin, is apt to go to pieces in being transferred. A gentle inclination of the warm plate is advantageous, so that a tendency may be given to the slice to slip downwards of itself on to the clean glass. We must never attempt to lift the slice. All shiftings of its position should be performed with the point of a long needle or other sharp instrument. If it goes to pieces we may yet be able to pilot the fragments to their resting place on the balsam of the new glass, and the resulting slide may be sufficient for the required purpose.

When the slice has been safely conducted to the centre of the glass slip, we put a little Canada balsam over it, and allow it to be warmed as before. Then taking with the forceps one of the well-cleaned thin cover-glasses, we allow it gradually to rest upon the slice by letting down first one side, and then by degrees the whole. A few gentle circular movements of the cover-glass with the point of the needle or the forceps may be needed to ensure the total disappearance of air-bubbles. When these do not appear, and when, as before, we find that the balsam has acquired the proper degree of consistence, the slide containing the slice is removed, and placed on the table with a small lead weight above it in the same way as already described. On becoming quite cold and hard the superabundant balsam round the edge of the cover-glass may be scraped off with a knife, and any which still adheres to the glass may be removed with a little spirits of wine.

Small labels should be kept ready for affixing to the slides to mark the locality and reference number of the

P

specimen.   Thus labelled the slide may be put away for future study and comparison.

The whole process seems perhaps a little tedious.   But in reality much of it is so mechanical that after the mode of manipulation has been learnt by a little experience, the rubbing-down may be done while the operator is reading.   Thus in the evening, when enjoying a pleasant book after his day in the field, he may at the same time with some practice rub down his rock-chips, and thus get over the drudgery of the operation almost unconsciously.

Boxes with grooved sides for carrying microscopic slides are sold in different sizes. Such boxes are most convenient for field-work, as they go into small space, and with the help of a little cotton-wool they hold the glass-slides firmly without risk of breakage.   For a final resting-place, a case with shallow trays or drawers in which the slides can lie flat is most convenient.

One final remark may here be required.   The learner must not suppose that having prepared his slices, he has nothing to do but to place them under the microscope and at once determine their composition.   He will find it by no means an easy task to make satisfactory progress, and at first he may be inclined to abandon microscopic work in despair of ever gaining confidence in it.   Let him, however, begin by studying individual minerals, and make himself acquainted gradually with their various characters.   He should procure numerous sections of minerals which enter into the composition of the rocks which he wishes to investigate.   By degrees he will be able to discriminate them as they occur in the rocks, and once able to do this, his progress will be comparatively smooth.   But he must be prepared for a long patient course of training, and ought on no account to speak confidently about the microscopic structure of rocks until he feels assured that the confidence arises from sound knowledge.

THE MICROSCOPE.

As already stated (*ante*, p. 30), it is not necessary to procure an expensive microscope with very high magnifying powers. For most purposes of the field-geologist the 1½-inch objective with a magnifying power of from 20 to 50 or 60 diameters, according to the eye-pieces employed, will be found the most generally useful. But he should also have an objective capable of giving, with suitable eye-piece combinations, magnification up to from 200 to 300 diameters. A nose-piece for both objectives screwed to the foot of the tube saves much time and trouble by enabling the observer at once to pass from a low to a high power. Two Nicol prisms are indispensable ; one of these is to be fitted below the stage, the other is most advantageously placed over the eye-piece. A quartz-plate is useful. It should be so arranged below the stage as to be conveniently slipped in and out of the field as required. The numerous small pieces of apparatus necessary for physiological work are not needed in the examination of rocks and minerals.

Reflected Light.—It is always desirable to observe the characters of a rock as an opaque object. This cannot usually be done with a broken fragment of the stone, except of course with very low powers. Hence one of the most useful preliminary examinations of a prepared slice is to place it in the field, and, throwing the mirror out of gear, to converge as strong a light upon it as can be had, short of bright direct sunlight.   The advantage of this method is more particularly noticeable in the case of opaque minerals.   The sulphides and iron oxides so abundant in rocks appear as densely black objects with transmitted light, and show only their external form.   But by throwing a strong light upon their surface we may often discover that they possess a distinct and character-istic internal structure.   Titaniferous iron is an admirable example of the advantage of this method.   Seen with transmitted light that mineral appears in black, utterly structureless grains or opaque patches, though frequently bounded by definite lines and angles.   But with re-flected light the cleavage and lines of growth of the mineral can then often be clearly seen, and what seemed to be uniform black patches are then found in many cases to inclose bright brassy kernels of pyrite.

Transmitted Light.—It is, of course, with the light allowed to pass through the prepared slices that most of the microscopic examination of minerals and rocks is performed.   A little experience will show the learner that in viewing objects in this way he may obtain some-what different results from two slices of the same rock according to their relative thinness.   In the thicker one a certain mineral will appear perhaps brown or almost black, while in the other what is evidently the same mineral may be pale yellow or green, or almost colour-less.

Dichroism.—Some minerals show a change of colour when a Nicol prism is rotated below them.   Hornblende, for example, exhibits a gradation from deep brown to dark yellow—a mineral presenting this change is said to

be dichroic. To ascertain the dichroism of any mineral
we remove the upper polarizing prism and leave only
the lower. If as we rotate the latter directly under the
stage of the microscope no change of tint can be observed, there is no dichroic mineral present, or at least
none which shows dichroism at the angle through which
it has been cut. But we may often detect little crystals
which offer a lively change of tone as the prism goes
round ; these are examples of dichroism. This behaviour
may be used to discriminate the mineral constituents of
rocks. Thus the two minerals hornblende and augite in
many respects resemble each other. They differ in their
cleavage angles, but these cannot always be found in
microscopic slices. Augite, however, remains passive or
nearly so while the lower prism is rotated : it is not
dichroic, or only very feebly so. Hornblende, on the
other hand, is very strongly dichroic.

Polarized Light.—By means of polarized light an
exceedingly delicate method of investigation is made
available. We use both the Nicol prisms. If the object
is a piece of glass, or an amorphous body, or a crystal
belonging to some substance which crystallizes in the
regular or cubic system, the light will reach our eye
unaffected by the intervention of the object. The field
will remain dark when the axes of the two prisms are
at right angles, in the same way as if no intervening
object were there. If however, the substance under
examination is a mineral belonging to one of the other
crystallographic systems, it will modify the polarized
beam of light. On rotating one of the prisms we
perceive bands or flashes of colour, and numerous
lines appear which before were invisible. The field

no longer remains dark when the two Nicol prisms are crossed.

It is evident, therefore, that we may readily tell by this means whether or not a rock contains any glassy con-stituent. If it does, then that portion of its mass will become dark when the prisms are crossed, while the crystalline parts will remain conspicuous by their bright-ness. A thin plate of quartz makes this separation of the glassy and crystalline parts of a rock even more satisfac-tory. It is placed under the stage, and the Nicol prisms are so adjusted with reference to it that the field of the microscope appears uniformly violet. The glassy portion of any rock placed on the stage will allow the violet light to pass through unchanged, but the crystalline portions will show other prismatic colours. The object should be rotated in the field and the eye kept steadily fixed upon one portion of the slide at a time, so that any change may be observed.

It would be far beyond the compass of this little hand-book to enter fully into the microscopic examination of rocks. The student who desires to pursue the subject further will find much assistance in the works quoted below.[1] For his satisfaction in the determination of rocks he may propound to himself the following questions :— 1st, Is the rock entirely crystalline, consisting solely of crystals of different minerals interlaced ; and if so, what are these minerals ? 2nd, Is there any trace of a glassy ground-mass? If there is he may remove the rock at once from the granite series. 3rd, Can he detect any evidence of the devitrification of what must have been

[1] Sorby "On the Microscopic Structure of Crystals, indicating the Origin of Minerals and Rocks," *Quart. Journ. Geo. Soc.* xiv.

at one time the glassy basis of the whole rock? This devitrification might be shown by the appearance of numerous microscopic hairs, rods, bundles of feather-like irregular or granular aggregations.   4th, In what order did the minerals crystallize? This may often be very clearly made out with the microscope, as, for instance, where one mineral is completely inclosed within another.   5th, What is the nature of any altera-tion which the rock may have undergone? In a vast number of cases the slices show abundant evidence of such metamorphism; felspar passing into a granular kaolin, augite changing into various indefinite green products termed " viridite," olivine into serpentine, while secondary calcite, quartz, and zeolites run in minute veins or fill up interstices of the rock.   6th, Is the rock a fragmental one ; and if so, what is the nature of its component grains? Is any trace of organic remains to be detected?

In fine, I return once more to the main purpose of this book, which is to induce the reader to cultivate geology as an out-of-door recreation, and to give him a few hints for his guidance.   Apart from its healthful mental training as a branch of ordinary education,

453; Zirkel's *Mikroskopische Beschaffenheit der Mineralien und Gesteine* (Leipzig, 1873) ; Rosenbusch's *Mikroskopische Physiographie der Mineralien und Gesteine*, 2 vols. (Stuttgart, 1873, 1876). [Since this note was in type an excellent manual on petrography by my friend Mr. F. Rutley, has been published by Messrs. Longman and Co.]

geology as an open-air pursuit affords an admirable training in habits of observation, furnishes a delightful relief from the cares and routine of every-day life, takes us into the open fields, and the free fresh face of nature, leads us into all manner of sequestered nooks, whither hardly any other occupation or interest would be likely to send us, sets before us problems of the highest interest regarding the history of the ground beneath our feet, and thus gives a new charm to scenery which may be already replete with attractions.   Even, therefore, should the reader never write a single sentence of geological description, nor venture to put one geological line upon a map, he may gain from the prosecution of field-geology many a happy and profitable hour, alike in the country into which the pursuit leads him, and in his own home with quiet reflection on what he has seen and done in the field.

INDEX.

INDEX.

RICHARD CLAY & SONS,
BREAD STREET HILL, LONDON, E.C.
And at Bungay, Suffolk.

www.ingramcontent.com/pod-product-compliance
Lightning Source LLC
Chambersburg PA
CBHW020113030726
47498CB00006B/2084